5/21

FEB 2 4 2021

ALSO BY ANNABEL LYON

The Sweet Girl
The Golden Mean

CONSENT

CONSENT

—

ANNABEL LYON

ALFRED A. KNOPF

NEW YORK

2021

THIS IS A BORZOI BOOK
PUBLISHED BY ALFRED A. KNOPF

Copyright © 2020 by Annabel Lyon

This is a work of fiction. Names, characters, places, and
incidents either are the product of the author's imagination
or are used fictitiously. Any resemblance to actual persons,
living or dead, events, or locales is entirely coincidental.

www.aaknopf.com

LIBRARY OF CONGRESS CATALOGING-IN-PUBLICATION DATA
Names: Lyon, Annabel, [date] author.
Title: Consent / Annabel Lyon.
Description: First edition. | New York : Alfred A.
Knopf, [2021] |
Identifiers: LCCN 2020009957 (print) |
LCCN 2020009958 (ebook) | ISBN 9780593318003 (hardcover) |
ISBN 9780593318010 (ebook) Subjects: LCSH: Domestic fiction.
Classification: LCC PR9199.3.L98 C66 2021 (print) |
LCC PR9199.3.L98 (ebook) | DDC 813/.6—dc23
LC record available at https://lccn.loc.gov/2020009957
LC ebook record available at https://lccn.loc.gov/2020009958

Front-of-jacket photograph: EyeEm / Getty Images
Jacket design by Kelly Blair

Printed in the United States of America
First United States Edition

CONSENT

The baby doesn't cry but Sara's mother cries. Everyone is tired and Sara is tired of playing nicely in the plash of sun on the carpet, the dust motes turning, while her mother feeds the baby and rocks the baby and mumbles into the phone, the swaddled baby in the crook of her arm. Sara misses the crook of her mother's arm and the smell of her, the honey-wood smell that comes from the faceted glass bottle on her dresser. She doesn't like the milk smell on her mother or the milk-shit smell on her sister.

Visitors wear brave watery smiles, and try to elicit brave watery smiles from Sara's mother. Something about the baby and the baby's placidity, Sara gathers, is not quite right. The baby is too quiet, the baby sleeps too much. People are gentle and kind and hand the baby back quickly to her mother, who does not rush to take her.

They bring big gifts for the baby and small gifts for

Sara, which is unfair and absurd and makes Sara impatient. Sticker sheets and socks and little books that she is encouraged to read to the baby, which is unfair. Sara can't read. She has to turn the pages by herself in the plash of sunlight, the dust motes spinning endlessly, because her mother cannot. She just cannot read to her right now.

When Sara's father comes home, Sara's mother goes to bed. Then her father holds the baby in the crook of his arm and scrambles Sara's eggs with one hand. He reads the new books with her and puts the baby on the floor more than Sara's mother does so he can play with Sara. She appreciates this. He smells sourer than her mother, and his cheek is rough. She doesn't want to shift allegiances, not really, but what choice does she have?

A chokingly sweet-smelling older woman comes to visit. Sara's *great-aunt*. That sounds very grand. She brings another pink bear for the baby but a big gift for Sara: a Barbie doll and a child's suitcase filled with clothes. Some of them are the cheap things that came with the doll, plastic netting crinolines and pink pretend silk dresses and white plastic shoes that snap onto her feet. But some were hand-sewn by the *great-aunt* herself for some distant child who is grown up now. Real silk, real velvet, real wool, even real fur: scraps from real fabrics used to make real clothes. The stitches are tiny, like an elf would make. Fur-trimmed hooded capes, rickrack edged gowns, little two-piece suits, a tiny bouclé pea-coat. Sara sits in her plash of sunlight, turning the little clothes this way and that, dressing and undressing the Barbie. She is a very good girl.

"That scent is roses," her mother tells her once the *great-aunt* has left. The difference between roses and her mother's honey-wood fascinates her. She sniffs back and forth from the doll's clothes to her mother's sleeve, again and again, trying to recapture the bursting surprise of a beautiful thing that has nothing of her mother in it. The next day her father brings her a little bottle of scent for her own self from the drugstore because her mother asked him to. Then she loves her mother again.

1 9 9 8

You're not the boss of me, they used to tell each other as children. Saskia and Jenny, Jenny and Saskia. Same size, same face, same stubbornness. Their own father couldn't reliably tell them apart until they were five. *You're not the boss of me.*

"Yes, twins," their mother would tell strangers who stopped to admire their dark eyes, their curls. Their mother was always smiling tiredly. She wasn't the boss, either, though she knew them better than their father. Knew them well enough that when she sat on the sofa as the afternoon light drained away, and Jenny would say, "Jenny's upstairs, Jenny's hurt," their mother would sip from her glass without looking at her and say, "That's very funny. Nice try."

"Really, I'm Saskia," Jenny would say.

"I'm resting, okay?" their mother would say. "Try to understand."

"She didn't fall for it," Jenny would tell Saskia upstairs,

where she lay on the bed, pretending to be Jenny. Saskia had known she wouldn't fall for it, but it was easier to let Jenny play her games.

"What do you want to do now?" Jenny would say, jumping up. "I know! Let's try on her clothes. We can put music on and dress up and pretend to—"

"I want to read."

"That's boring. Play with me. You have to play with me or I'll set your book on fire."

She would, too, in the bathroom sink, with the barbeque lighter. She had got a spanking last time, but it would not deter her from doing it again. Only Saskia could save her, by giving in. That was her one power. Still: "You're not the boss of me!"

A lie. Jenny always got what she wanted, always. She could twist Saskia into any trouble she wanted.

Jenny's eyes sparkled. Saskia was serious. *That* was how you told them apart.

PART ONE

CHAPTER ONE

Fall 1992

When the letter came, Sara took it straight to her mother.

"The University of Toronto," her mother said.

"Yes."

"Do you hate us?"

There was money, a burst of money from the death of the great-aunt the year before. Now her mother was crying into the sink.

"I'll come back," Sara said.

Then it was August and she was on a plane.

"Eighteen," the man next to her said. "I remember eighteen. What are you going to study?"

"French."

"*Magnifique,* honey," the man said.

He was from Squamish, and was going to Toronto for a business opportunity. Something to do with resorts, with skiing. He personally didn't ski, but.

"Oh, interesting!" Sara said. She opened her magazine.

"Eighteen," the man said again, but Sara was reading.

The magazine was *The New Yorker*. The article was about Proust. Sara had a *Vogue* in her bag, too, and a granola bar: breakfast. It was a 7:00 a.m. flight.

"Oh, you do not want to be an interpreter," her mother had said. "Since when? You've only ever wanted to teach music, since you were little."

Sara had not wanted to teach music since before her father's death, from a heart attack, when she was ten. "With French I could go into government. The foreign service. Law." Though, in truth, she had already decided to go into fashion. What did that mean? She wasn't sure. She hated the mall. She wasn't pretty. It had something to do with taste, money and taste and books and, of course, eros. She had another book in her bag, one she was ashamed of and couldn't read in public, even with her mother and sister dwindled to pinpoints thirty thousand feet below and behind her.

They landed mid-afternoon Toronto time. The man next to her wished her luck, and asked her if she had a place to stay.

"With friends," she lied.

She'd won the school prizes for French and English back in June, but had lost calculus and the sciences to her friend David Park. At the prize ceremony he had performed one of his own compositions on the violin and received the school's top graduating scholarship. Sara had got a scholarship, too, for $150, and a hardcover dictionary stamped with the school crest.

"You should play with me," David had said beforehand.

"Accompany you," Sara corrected him.

"I hate that word. The parts are equally difficult." David was the child of immigrants who spoke Korean at home and relied on him to be their link to the new world. He suffered the classic schisms Sara had read of in novels: the conflicting loyalties, the alienation, the guilt.

"I get too nervous," Sara said.

He shook his head. "You don't practice enough."

They went out a handful of times the summer after graduation. Sometimes they took Mattie with them, to the free lunchtime concerts in the art gallery, or the movies if it was a matinee and a comedy. Afterwards David Park would stay for supper. Sara's mother tried Chinese recipes on him—chicken with peeled almonds, strange yellow curries—that she'd never made before and never would again. They weren't good. Her mother also spoke to him too loudly and slowly, and would always bleach the bathroom after he'd left for the evening. But he was polite and Mattie adored him, holding his hand most everywhere they went, which he claimed not to mind. Sara suggested increasingly forbidding outings—a Cindy Sherman exhibit, Kieślowski's *The*

Decalogue at the Pacific Cinémathèque—so that they'd have a reason to leave Mattie at home.

He drove her home after the Cinémathèque and, as she was removing her seat belt, asked if he might kiss her. Dry lips, mint—some anticipatory candy or other. So that was out of the way. She was leaving in two days.

"I'll keep an eye on Mattie for you while you're away," he said. But Sara had no intention of returning either to her mother's pious bigotry or to the life of self-improvement that dating David Park entailed. She told him there was really no need for him to do that.

She had booked a room for a week at a budget hotel with a free airport shuttle, downtown, near Maple Leaf Gardens. Her hotel room was a smoking, not what she had requested, with a mustard-coloured duvet. She spent a while thinking about mustard colour, and whether it wasn't worse than cigarette smell. Really she was avoiding having to go out and get a newspaper and something to eat. She was afraid to leave the room.

She took her secret book to the bathroom and locked the door. It was a memoir by a woman who had worked as an editor at French *Vogue*. She was classy and acid and opinionated. One did not collect T-shirts; one owned pieces. One wore perfume, like a grown-up, and had an ongoing relationship with a competent tailor. The author peppered the book with reminiscences of her childhood in Saigon and then Paris, of watching her mother buy clothes, have them altered, have them cleaned, and finally get ready to go out in them for the evening. Her parents were not unreasonably wealthy, but her mother had taste and chic, and would rather have one expensive scarf than five cheap ones. That, the author said, was the correct attitude, the correct approach. Even after her charming rake of a half-British father had drunk up the family money and deposited her and her mother in a seedy hotel while he pursued increasingly nebulous business opportunities, her mother had kept her priorities straight. She had sold the paintings and the first editions, but not the Diors. Fortunately, by then, the author was old enough to pass as old enough to model, and soon she and her mother were comfortable again. (Her father had gone to work as a Hollywood screenwriter, and had started another family there. The author never saw him again.)

If a fourteen-year-old could support her family, Sara could leave her awful room. At a corner store she bought a *Star* for the rental listings. She walked on down the street, stomach growling. She'd adored the chapter on the editor's affair with the famous perfumer, and wanted to reread it with something to eat.

Months later she would walk the same sidewalks, now through slush like filthily gravied and peppered mashed potato. She had found a room in a decrepit mansion in the Annex, a mansion subdivided and rented to students like herself. In her room she had a bed and desk and chair, a fridge and a hotplate and a toaster. She ate a lot of toast. By now—early December—she had her routines. She woke early to a frugal breakfast and went to class. Then she went to the library. There were two or three cafés she would choose between for her afternoon coffee. There were three or four used bookstores she cycled through each week, and then of course there was Simenon.

The bell above the door tinkled. There was a bell above the door. That was Simenon: stained glass at your knees, then seven steps below the street and a bell above the door. Silks and furs and dust in the wavering blue-green stained-glass light. The assistants down there were mermaids, drifting green and lovely through the gloom, but their queen was the one Sara feared and hoped for: a hag not five feet tall with the ugliest face, gaping drooping mouth too wide and eyes like kelp bulbs. She was probably younger than she looked. The first time Sara saw her, she assumed the woman was homeless. It took a closer look to notice her ripped black coat was Comme des Garçons and there were pheasant feathers on her shoes. Her glasses—when she put them on to sit at the ormolu desk and handwrite a receipt—had spiked rims.

She smelled of pepper and smoke, not a perfume in the conventional sense.

"Ne touchez pas, Mademoiselle," she had said the first time Sara visited the shop and reached for a price tag. Her eyes skimmed over Sara, her demure September skirt and sweater. By October the woman watched while Sara fingered this and that, finger and thumb only, never overstaying. It helped that she wore the vintage wool peacoat she'd bought from one of the mermaids on her first visit to prove herself, or at least to prove the reach of her wallet. November had been a dung-coloured silk scarf. When she returned the following week, the queen noticed she'd cut off the tassels.

"I didn't like them," Sara said. *"Je ne les ai pas aimé."*

"I do not know why we do not speak the one language or the other," the queen said. "I speak to you in English, you attempt French. Why?"

Sara touched a silk blouse with one finger.

"That is too small for you, Mademoiselle."

She touched another.

"That one also."

The queen went away and came back with a hideous green-and-orange knit dress that would have cost Sara a month's rent.

"This is for you," the queen said.

She was waiting on Sara herself. That had never happened before. Sara felt rather than saw the mermaids at the periphery of the store, behind the racks, hiding in the seaweed.

The queen walked into the change room with her and told her what to take off. She would not allow Sara to handle the thing, but dressed her herself and fussed over the buttons. When Sara reached to tug the fabric under one arm, the queen practically slapped her hand away and fixed it herself. She smoothed the fabric over Sara's hips and breasts with both hands, briskly, professionally, and stood back to examine her.

"Ce n'est pas mon goût," Sara said.

The queen led her from the change room to the shop, where she stood Sara in front of the big mirror. The mermaids drifted over. The queen murmured under her breath to one of them, who nodded. Sara understood they were disparaging her shoes. Her eyes went to the rack the queen kept behind her desk, where she kept her rarest pearls: a Poiret cocoon coat, a bias-cut gown from Madame Grès, a leather harness and leash from Vivienne Westwood. And something new: a black dress.

"What's that?" Sara asked.

The queen nodded at one of the mermaids, who retrieved the black dress and held it just out of Sara's reach. She reached anyway, then let her arm fall.

The queen nodded, and the mermaid came closer.

Sara reached again, but hesitated. "That's a deWinter."

The queen flicked her chin, and the mermaid returned the dress to the rack behind the desk.

"I've read about that dress," Sara said. "I've seen the photos."

They returned to the change room, where the queen supervised her undressing.

"I want to try it on," Sara said.

The queen left her in the change room, bearing away the green-and-orange knit dress. Sara stood for a long time in her underwear, waiting.

When she finally came out, the queen had rung up the hideous dress and was wrapping it in black tissue. Sara wondered if this was the price of trying on the deWinter. It worked like that down here—the queen read her mind and set her tests. Three tests: the peacoat, the scarf, and now this thing.

Sara paid and took the now-familiar Simenon bag. "I want to try it on," she repeated, instead of saying goodbye.

La petite rouge and *la petite noire,* that's what they were called in the spring of 1971. The designer was the legendary Paul Destry; the dresses came from one of his final collections. He was interested in the physics of clothing, planes and curves in motion. He had always been melancholic and disappointed in his own work. He refused all interviews, even after the dresses became famous, and subsequently abandoned fashion to dedicate his last years to mathematics. Shortly before his death in 1974, in the *Journal de Mathématiques Pures et Appliquées,* he published an article on the configuration of ferns, a little-known precursor to Mandelbrot's 1980 articulation of fractal geometry.

The red was the popular one. It was a boat-neck shift, slightly asymmetrical and severely cut. The drop from shoulder to hem was sheer. And yet it flattered, oddly; according to Sara's secret book, Saint Laurent himself was supposed to have bought one just to slit the seams and see where the curves were hidden. The red was rubies in blood. Women got married in it; women wanted to be buried in it. The black was less popular. People found it harsh.

The dress fell out of fashion abruptly, in August of 1971, when the photographer Paul deWinter was arrested for the rape and murder of one of his models. They had just finished a shoot inspired by Persephone in the underworld. The model was seventeen and didn't know the myth. She looked like a baby owl. DeWinter berated her for being old and fat, then followed her home and ate pomegranate with his coffee for breakfast the next morning, the very pomegranate from the shoot, while her body cooled in the next room. He then photographed the corpse: the model's own *petite noire* pushed up to the waist, thumb-bruises on the throat. There: Persephone in hell.

The photos were shown at trial and the dress got its name. French intellectuals claimed the photos as art. French women held chic parties to burn their deWinters. It was the seventies. Ten years later, the dress had a brief revival on the London punk scene, for the shock value. Then it disappeared.

Black was a child's idea of sophistication, the author wrote. An American's idea. The little black dress—stupid! Coco Chanel was a peasant. For her mother's funeral, the author made a point of wearing white, like a Viet woman. It was a philosophical issue. The author approved of the *petite rouge,* and wore hers even after the scandal. What had the dress done? she wanted to know. Nothing, that was what. Then, unsentimentally, she had sold the dress to a collector. Probably a fetishist, a pervert. He'd paid through the nose, anyway.

That was all right, Sara thought. She had her inheritance. She, too, could pay through the nose.

"Have you booked your ticket?" her mother asked on the phone.

It was early evening in Toronto, mid-afternoon in Vancouver. A three-hour difference. Sara lay on her bed, holding the phone to her ear. "Not yet."

"I'll book it for you if you give me your dates."

"No," Sara said. "I mean, I'll do it."

"No *thank you*," her mother said.

"How's Mattie?" Sara asked. Her mother sighed. Sara stretched and yawned mightily, silently. "I'll book a ticket tomorrow." *I'll try the deWinter tomorrow.*

"How are your classes?"

"Good. Classes are good."

"I hope you're picking up a proper accent." Her mother spoke just enough honeymoon French to correct Sara and Mattie when they pronounced the final *t* in "croissant." "Proper" meant "not Québécois."

"One of my professors studied at the Sorbonne."

"Did he?" Sara could hear her mother's pleasure.

"She. How's Mattie?"

"The same. *Her* accent must be lovely. What does she teach?"

"Actually, I owe her a paper tomorrow," Sara said. "On Jean Genet. I have her for theatre."

"You're studying theatre now?"

"French theatre," Sara said. "It's still French."

"David will be happy to see you," her mother said. "He's taken Mattie out quite a few times since you've been gone. To the movies, mostly."

"Has he?" Sara said. "That's nice of him."

"I tease her about her gentleman caller. If it were anyone but an Oriental I wouldn't encourage it, but those people—"

"All right," Sara said.

"They're known for their propriety, at least. He'll be wanting to pick up where you left off, I suppose?"

"Not necessarily."

Her mother sighed again. Sara detected relief. "You need to see him at least once. To thank him for all the time he's spent with Mattie. Those people are very particular about observing the courtesies."

Sara did not say *which people?*

"You'll put a stop to it," her mother said. "Mattie will miss him, but that can't be helped."

After she said goodbye to her mother, Sara reread the chapter set in Saigon, the chapter about the author's torrid affair with a Chinese man before the war. They would contrive to send each other notes—*cet après-midi à cinq heures,* left in the toe of a shoe—and the author would lie to her mother and sneak away to get fucked. She was fourteen. The chapter was a catalogue of clothing torn: silk torn, satin torn, muslin torn, schoolgirl-cotton torn. She mended these clothes herself with her little sewing kit, tiny stitches like an elf would make. If her mother noticed, she didn't let on. He masturbated her so long and hard she got a blister on her clitoris. He once bit her breast so she bled—skin torn—and then that too became a game.

There were lessons there, the author wrote. Skin as

fabric, fabric as armour. The hot soup of sex and love and fear. Clothes as costume and code. Her prose became vague here, in the philosophical French way, lyrical and explicit and willing to shock, yet vague and repetitive, obsessive.

Sara decided she would see David Park as soon as she got back to Vancouver, just as her mother had requested.

The day after her phone call with her mother, Sara returned to Simenon.

"It will not fit you," the queen said.

"It will." Three months of toast.

"You are too tall."

"I'm not."

"You can't afford it."

Sara didn't deign to answer that one.

"It's a museum piece."

"It's a dress."

The queen flicked a finger irritably at one of the mermaids, who fetched the deWinter and bore it to the change room on both arms. Again, the queen entered with Sara. She stripped to her underwear, but the queen flicked her finger.

"You know the name of the dress, but not how to wear it," she said. "You must be naked. That is how this dress is worn."

"I know."

"You know because I tell you."

Sara stripped off her bra and panties and allowed the queen to shiver the dress over her raised arms, her breasts, her hips. It was clinging and cold.

"Ha," the queen said. She looked unhappy.

Sara did not buy the deWinter on that visit, or the next. She stayed away from Simenon for a couple of weeks and when she returned she pretended she was over it. But the queen knew. Sara had come just before closing on a Saturday, on a whim, hot like a fuck-addled school-girl who couldn't stay away any longer. The queen looked at her over the top of her spiked glasses and said, *"Alors."*

First, though, there would be wine. One of the mermaids locked the door and turned the sign around while the other got a bottle of crémant and glasses. They would be closed Sunday and Monday and it was their habit, the queen said, to toast the coming weekend. Sara was invited to join them.

"Cherches-là," the queen said to the first mermaid, who fetched the dress and laid it across Madame's desk where they could all consider it while they drank. The bubbles bit tenderly at Sara's tongue. This was not champagne, only sparkling. Sara knew without knowing

that there was champagne in that back room also, only not for her. Probably caviar, too, and cheese veined with edible gold, and pâté of brandy and prune and human baby, to be nibbled on water crackers. Not for her, even though she was buying the dress today, and they were celebrating.

Now the queen asked the mermaid named Ghislaine to refill their glasses, and the mermaid named Élodie took a large book from beneath Madame's desk and opened it to a black and white photograph of the model Annick M. wearing the red deWinter. Sara stood beside her and they leafed through the big glossy book together, while Élodie exhaled tinily at each photo. She couldn't imagine what kind of room this exquisite creature could possibly go home to. Maybe she lived in the back of the shop with the champagne. Maybe she and Ghislaine subsisted on grapes and Veuve Clicquot and swing-danced together in the shop at midnight and serviced each other with their pink tongues after, and slept on fox furs.

The bottle was empty. Ghislaine opened another. Sara was drinking too much, but not more than the others, she thought. The queen pushed her glasses up onto her hair to squint at the radio on her desk. She adjusted the dial and sounds fell like raindrops. Not swing at all, but a complex, rhythmic, pentatonic plinking. Sara could hear the musicians' fingertips on the drums, the slight adhesion before the release. She could hear everything.

"Gamelan," the queen said, to her enquiring look. "From Indonesia."

It was decided, not with words, that Sara would try the dress on again. She turned to the change room but the queen said, "No, why?" So she stripped there in front of everyone and let them ease the dress over her head, all three together, and then there was more wine, and the question of shoes, and it was decided there were no suitable shoes in the shop, but Ghislaine or was it Élodie found a catalogue and searched until she found a picture the queen approved, and a call was made to put them on hold for Sara, who swore she would buy only them and the next day did, and Élodie or was it Ghislaine, the one with the brown eyes tinged with red-gold, helped her back into her own clothes while the queen sat at the desk and handwrote a receipt for an amount that Sara could have spent on a trip to Paris (she had been costing this out, recently, wondering if she could pull it off without having to tell her mother), and then they were helping her back up the stairs and pushing her gently out into the night, colder now than when she had come, saying they would have the dress delivered to her, one did not carry a dress like that in a bag through the street like a common piece of shopping, and then Sara was walking into the night with the queen's instructions echoing behind her, *drink a large glass of water when you get home,* for Sara was drunk, though not too drunk to understand that they were afraid of her losing the dress in the back of a taxi. That irony would remain with her through the long future of her addiction: that she would continue to understand people long after she had lost the capacity to speak without slurring or make herself, in any remotely attractive way, understood.

The photographer Paul deWinter (claimed the author of Sara's pillow book) was a close friend of the dress's designer, Destry, a portly little bespectacled fellow indistinguishable from a thousand other portly little bespectacled fellows from wartime photographic portraits, except that he was a genius with a surname that might as well have been Couture. The author had met them both and found them eerily intimate with each other, and largely aloof with everyone else. Not sexual intimacy, but something stranger, stronger. (Stronger than sex? Sara had wondered, youngly.) Eerie because they belonged to different eras, though the designer couldn't have been more than ten years older than the photographer. Black and white versus colour; cravat versus love beads; alligators versus espadrilles; plumply smooth-shaven versus nailed-Jesus lean. Nineteen-fifties versus nineteen-sixties; genial versus impulsive, mannered versus crude, and so on and on. You could be that simplistic, the author said, if you wanted. But it was the similarities that *she* noticed the day of *her* photo shoot, two years before the murder. A penis in the pants was a penis in the pants, and a man screaming at you by the swimming pool of a private villa was a man screaming at you, whether he was pinning you or lighting you up. Their eyes burned, both of them. M. Couture smoked. Well, they both smoked, but Paul deWinter had a needle and a spoon too. M. Couture was, by that time, terminally ill. He coughed yellow clots into a hanky, died just a couple of years later, and was accorded a state funeral. His hands were soft and he sewed her into the dress by hand, gently. It was (she recalled) grey, and ethereally ruffled. Paul deWinter, with his ugly Dutch accent, was sulky because she wasn't a blonde, but he got the job done; got her a cover, in fact. She looked like a bird. It was 1969. The murdered girl was a blonde.

"But their strangeness!" the author wrote. "I will give you an example. During the shoot, Paul took a phone call, from the elder brother in Rotterdam, it turned out. (There had been three deWinter brothers: the youngest, everyone's favourite, had died in a motorcycle crash. The eldest was a staid professor of early music. Paul was the middle child.) Come home, the music professor said, *Moeder* is dying. I knew this because Paul hung up the phone and told us right away and the two of them smiled and shrugged in perfect understanding. It was regrettable, but it was not possible. No *moeder,* dead or alive, was going to interrupt their work."

Sara landed in Vancouver on a December afternoon. She had wanted to take a taxi to the West side, to extend her solitude by those twenty minutes, but her mother and sister were waiting inside the terminal. Sara knew what it had cost her mother to suffer the price of airport parking. Both their faces lit when they saw her, her sister's with joy, her mother's with joy and hellfire. Mattie ran to her and gave her a long hug, then stroked the arm of Sara's green-and-orange dress appreciatively.

"Yes, new," Sara said.

She hugged her mother, and then the three of them went to wait at the luggage carousel. Her mother insisted on procuring a cart, and fussed over the arrangement of their coats and purses on it while they waited.

"All of it?" her mother asked that evening, after Mattie had gone to bed and they were sitting in the living room. Sara had refused the sherry her mother had offered her—though she wanted it—because it was sherry, and because it implied permission. The tiny glass of blood in her mother's hand looked good now, though.

"Most of it."

She had expected her mother to cry, or yell. But by the time she went to bed, Sara had merely agreed to move back into her old room and begin courses at the University of British Columbia the following September. She would have the spring and summer to, as her mother put it, "recover herself."

"You'll have to give us a fashion show," her mother said as Sara leaned down to kiss her soft cheek goodnight. "Mattie and me."

David Park would not have sex with her, though he was breathing hard. "You aren't yourself," he told her.

"I'm more myself than before I left."

They were sitting in his car, the very next evening.

"You spent your inheritance on clothes?" he said. "How is that even possible?"

"Think of it like art." Sara smoothed the silk of her skirt over her thighs, reached to put her seat belt back on. David started the engine. "Like if you spent all your money going to concerts."

"Then I'd be an idiot. Plus, it's not art. It's clothes."

Sara looked at her lap.

David reached across her to open the glove compartment. He pulled out an envelope and gave it to her. "I'm giving a benefit concert tomorrow. My church is organizing a fundraiser for new immigrants. I want you to bring your family."

"Thank you." Sara looked at the tickets in the envelope, politely. "I'll be sure to wear something nice."

After the performance, Sara's mother bundled Mattie into her coat, pulling it tightly around her. Anger crackled between Sara and her mother, but then David came over and they had to pretend they'd had a lovely evening. They spoke for a few moments about the program. Sara's mother said she recalled seeing Itzhak Perlman perform the Sarasate in London in the eighties, and compared David's performance favourably to that one. David kissed Mattie's cheek, making her blush. When David left them to greet other acquaintances, they went outside. Other families lingered on the sidewalk, exchanging wishes for the new year. When their cab came, Sara helped her mother and sister in and then slammed the door. She knew her mother had been expecting her to go home with them; had been waiting for the privacy of the car to resume their argument. Sara went back into the church foyer, drank two overpriced plastic cups of cold red wine too quickly, so that by the time David was free of his admirers and relations she felt soft and ready for him. But he wasn't smiling. "What was Mattie wearing?"

Sara shrugged.

"She looked ridiculous." David handed Sara her coat, but didn't help her with it. "Everyone was staring. You could see her—everything, underneath. She must have been freezing."

"That's how you wear it. It's a famous dress." Sara told him the story of it as they walked to his car. "Mattie has no idea," she added. "She was just thrilled to wear it."

"She's thrilled any time you're nice to her. Which isn't very often. Did you think you were being funny?"

"Perlman's vibrato was a little much. You know, that Jewish schmaltz. Yours was just perfect."

"What's your point? That you're not an anti-Semite like your mother, so it's okay? It's not okay. That was an evil thing you did to Mattie tonight. Someday you'll know better."

"She loves you." Sara looked dully out the window at the familiar streets. She understood he was driving her home. "She told me once she wanted to marry you."

"I could do worse." David pulled to the curb in front of her house and leaned across her to open the door. "If I could stay friends with her without ever seeing you or your mother—"

Sara went inside. The house was dark and quiet. She

stopped in the kitchen to pour herself a juice tumbler of her mother's wine and took it upstairs. Mattie's room was next to hers and she paused in the open doorway, as was her habit, to check the curtains were closed, the room wasn't too cold, and the humidifier was topped up. Mattie suffered sleep apnea and was vulnerable to bronchial infections, particularly in winter.

She was sleeping hard, mouth open, soft curls awry on the pillow. The dress, Sara knew, would be hung back in her own closet. She would straighten the shoulder seams ever so slightly to make it her own again, and then she'd go to bed herself. But for now she touched the glass to her lips, then lifted the glass higher so she could graze her wrist with her nose. She was wearing scent, cardamom and musk—expensive, French—that she'd been saving for this date with David. She watched her sister's pretty stillness, her rosebud mouth, her chest that rested a fraction too long before her breath caught and, with an endearing snuffle, she breathed again.

Earlier that evening they'd sat together in Sara's room, looking at Sara's new clothes. Mattie didn't understand or care that they were shamefully expensive, only that they were soft (the cashmeres) or shiny (the silks) or pretty (the orange-and-green dress).

"That's not really pretty, Mats," Sara said. "It's pretty ugly, actually."

"Orange is pretty," Mattie corrected her. Sara stood Mattie in front of the mirror and helped her into the peacoat. The sleeves swallowed her fingertips. Sara tried pushing them up, but Mattie frowned. "That's sloppy."

"Not always." Sara resented her mother's ability to throw her voice into her sister. "Here, try this one."

Eventually they settled on a robin's egg blue cashmere with short sleeves. "That's for you," Sara said.

Mattie's eyes flared with pleasure. "For Christmas?"

"For right now."

Mattie giggled.

"It matches your eyes. Mummy will like it."

Mattie kept the sweater in her lap to stroke like a kitten while Sara returned to the closet. "Your favourite colour is black," Mattie said. "Why do you wear so much black?"

Fury forked across the night sky of Sara's mind. Impulsively, angrily, generously, vengefully, fondly, coldly, she had unzipped the deWinter from its garment bag.

CHAPTER TWO

October 2011

At the funeral, Mattie and Sara held hands. They accepted condolences together with a grave grace. Many of the mourners told them they had never seemed more alike, or like their mother. Afterwards they hosted a reception at the house, Sara offering drinks and Mattie methodically approaching each guest with a tray of hors d'oeuvres, vegetables frilled with cream cheese that she herself had piped.

After their guests had left and they had tidied the house, Sara asked Mattie if she would like to watch one of her movies.

"Will you watch with me?" Mattie asked.

It was dusk. Sara stood by the arm of the sofa, watching the men and women on the screen sing and dance in their flounced dresses and fancy pants. Every night for the past week she had stayed in her old room, listening to Mattie cry herself to sleep. Sara wanted wine. She wanted salmon sashimi. She wanted her laptop on her lap—her work—in her own chair in her own living room, with her own view into the lit, stacked living rooms of the high-rise across the street and the other single lives being profitably led there. She would have to sell the house, soon, and find Mattie somewhere to live. A group home, with staff to care for her, and friends who liked the same things she did.

"You're hovering," Mattie said. "You're making me nervous." This was something their mother used to say.

Sara perched on the edge of the sofa.

"Sit *back*."

Sara stood up. "Will you be all right on your own tonight?"

The musical number concluded with the entire cast striking an exuberant pose. Then everyone relaxed and the dialogue resumed as though it had never stopped. Mattie turned away from the television and met Sara's eyes with a bleak look in which neither intelligence nor the lack of it had a place.

Robert was the handyman. He did odd jobs around the neighbourhood: replaced the furnace filter, unstopped the antique upstairs toilet, cleaned the gutters, put up shelves. When Sara had helped her mother with the household accounts at the end of every month, there had always been some little sum for Robert, nothing she had ever questioned. Now her mother was gone less than a month and Mattie had phoned to say she and Robert were married.

"No, Mattie," Sara had said. "You're not married."

Mattie had invited her for supper, to come see.

You are unkind, their mother had told Sara, not long before her heart attack. *I am not trying to smother you. You would have your own rooms here, your own office, everything you could want. You can even have your meals on a tray when you are busy with your work. You know what is coming as well as I do. Why do you fight it?*

As Sara parked her car in front of the big old house, she recalled the only time she had met Robert, the previous spring. She had been getting out of the car just as she was now when he had come around the side of the house with a mangled squirrel on a shovel.

"Sara Landow." She stepped onto the lawn, extending her hand. He set the shovel down and they had shook, both of them strong-gripped, wary. He was her age, late-thirties, with ginger hair cropped close to his skull, thin lips, pale blue eyes. She intuited a dark, bitter sense of humour, and a matching strain of intelligence.

"Ms. Landow." He nodded. "The older sister, the professor."

She suffered his clear, pale-eyed look, conscious of her silk shirt, suede skirt, wool coat, French perfume, Italian leather boots. She wondered what else he knew: about her failure to marry; about her work, and the long, steady ascent of her career; about her ongoing refusal to move "home" and help with Mattie's care. He had not offered his own name. He explained about the squirrel, that Mattie and Mrs. Landow had found it that morning on the back deck, blood everywhere, and called him in a bit of a tizzy. His word. A cat had got it, he thought. A coyote wouldn't have left so much behind. She watched him add it to the curbside trash can. "Now for the blood," he said, and for the next hour or so, while she drank tea with her family and received a fuller recapitulation of the discovery of the poor, poor squirrel, she was aware of him whistling and scrubbing the back deck, occasionally stopping to sip from the mug Mattie had carefully carried out to him. When he was done he rapped on the kitchen window and waved to let them know he was leaving. The deck—Sara had checked—was spotless.

Now it was November. She parked next to five clear plastic bags of leaves, and when she got out of the car smelled smoke in the air, pleasantly. Then she noticed it was coming from the Landow chimney.

"Mattie!" She ran through the front door. She could see her sister squatting on her heels in front of the hearth, firelight dancing on her face. "Mattie, get back."

Mattie looked up at her, astonished.

"You must never—"

Robert came through from the kitchen in sock feet, holding a drink. "Sara. Don't worry about the chimney, I had it swept last week. Dinner won't be long. We made roast beef to celebrate, didn't we, Mattie-Battie? Roast beef?"

Mattie stood up and put her arm around his waist. He kissed her hair and looked back at Sara, waiting to see what she would do.

"She showed me the marriage licence," Sara told the lawyer the next day.

Mattie was fine by herself at night and could do simple meals and baking, tea and toast, soup from a can, grilled cheese, salad, pudding, cookies even. She had her bus pass. During the day she had her job at the workshop and her crafts at the drop-in centre. At night she watched movies and talked with her workshop friends on the phone. Sara usually called her once or twice each day to make sure she was all right, and visited three or four times a week to help with cleaning and shopping, and to keep her company now that their mother was no longer there. Mattie couldn't drive a car or concentrate on a book and she needed help with bigger sums of money, but in a short interaction with her you would not necessarily know these things. She was sweet and friendly and wore expensive nice clothes chosen by Sara and their mother.

Robert, though, she told the lawyer, would have known.

Mattie Landow had become Martha Dwyer. She had done it last week, while Sara had been at a three-day conference in Seattle.

The lawyer, a woman her own age, asked what kind of conference it was.

"Medical ethics," Sara said. "I'm an ethicist."

The lawyer asked if Sara or her mother had ever had Mattie declared legally incompetent.

"No. We would have had to go through a judge. We thought it would be humiliating for her. She can do so many things. We didn't see any reason to define her by what she couldn't do."

Sara explained that she had got Mattie on a wait-list for assisted living and was hopeful she'd get a place early in the new year. After that, she was planning to sell the house and use some of the money to take Mattie somewhere extra nice for vacation. California, maybe. Mattie would enjoy Universal Studios.

The lawyer would later tell her Robert Dwyer had a petty criminal record going back to juvie. Shoplifting, DUI, bad cheques, marijuana, like that. She explained that if Sara had her sister declared incompetent they could get the marriage annulled. Criminal charges were another matter.

"You mean fraud, theft?" Sara was thinking of her mother's assets. Mattie had her own bank account, enough for groceries and DVDs while their mother was ill, which she could more or less manage on her own, but the larger financial picture—investments and property taxes and so on—Sara handled. She was pretty sure everything was still all right there.

"I mean assault," the lawyer said.

After dinner Robert had taken her aside. He had said he knew the situation was a shock, and if it helped ease her mind he would be happy to leave the sisters alone and return in the morning. Mattie's face had fallen when they had told her Robert had to be away overnight.

"Where does he sleep?" Sara had asked when he was gone and she had locked all the doors and windows behind him. Mattie had blushed and laughed and hidden her face in her hands. Sara had never seen her so happy, so—that unavoidable word—radiant.

"Sexual assault," the lawyer said.

"You cannot love her," Sara said.

She sat with her sister's husband in her mother's kitchen. Mattie was watching a Danny Kaye movie a couple of rooms away. They could hear the regular, inarticulate burble of voices and the odd burst of music when Mattie boosted the volume for a song she liked.

"No," Robert said. "I won't pretend. But I like her a lot, and she's fond of me. We get along better than most couples, I'll guarantee you that. I don't mind how she is."

Sara said nothing. Those eyes again, pale and canny. Intelligence like an intimacy between them.

"I'm going to guess you've been a busy girl," Robert said. "I'm going to guess you've found out a few things about me. That's fine. Clean and straight for the last eighteen months—that's on my record too—but I'm guessing that's not foremost in your mind right now. That's fine. It's good to get these things out in the open. Mattie knows what kind of person I am, I've told her as much as she can understand. If it doesn't bother her, I'm going to suggest it shouldn't bother you."

"I could have brought the police with me today. That would have been my right. It was recommended to me, in fact."

"Jesus." He shook his head. "Why?"

"Why? Because she has the capacity of a child. She can't consent to any of this, not legally. Not to marriage. Not to—"

Mattie came into the kitchen and asked if anyone else wanted juice.

"Just for you, I think, Mattie-Battie," Robert said. "Good movie?"

"It's my favourite. Next time you have to watch with me."

"You know I will."

"I know," Mattie said.

When she was gone, Robert said, "You think I raped her? You think I'm a violent man? Look around. Do you see a mess in this house? Do you see anything missing, anything out of place? I cleaned the toilets this morning. I raked the lawn, I made the beds. In a little while I'm going to start dinner. I've helped Mattie comb her hair and cut her toenails. Clean and straight, it's all clean and straight."

Sara told him about the possibility of an annulment and a restraining order.

"You think I should get a lawyer, Sara? Is that what you would do, if you were me?" He seemed genuinely to want to know.

Sara shook her head, then nodded.

"Can you recommend someone?"

She said nothing.

"Sure you can. I'm sure you know more than one lawyer. I'm sure that's the kind of friends you have. I'm sure you get together with your lady lawyer friends for cappuccinos."

Lattes, Sara thought.

"All right. I'm not going to make fun of you. I'm not stupid, though. I want you to know that."

"No, you're not stupid. Mattie's the stupid one."

He leaned back in his chair. "That's an ugly way to talk."

From the TV room they heard Mattie laugh.

"Can I tell you a little bit about myself, Sara? Can I? You've established some things already in your mind, I can see that. That I have a criminal record. That I waited to get married until you were out of town. That I'm living here in this beautiful house and maybe that's fouling it for you. Am I warm?"

"It's not the house."

"All right! It's not the house. Now we're getting somewhere. Tell me, Sara, tell me what it is. Let's talk about it and see if we can work it out. I can tell you I didn't go to university. Is that it? Do you hate me because I watch the Discovery Channel?"

"Stop."

"My first wife had a master's in social work. I have a sister in the Kootenays and two nieces. Information, information. What else can I give you? I have high blood pressure. I take pills for it. When I was a kid I had a cat named Leo and a dog named Booker. My trade is carpentry. My favourite wood is cedar. I've been fired from every job I've ever had because I can't stand being told what to do. My bosses were always genuinely regretful. They knew my work was good but they didn't like the way I talked back and made them look bad in front of the crew. That's not trouble, that's self-respect. Drinking is what gets me in trouble, and I don't drink anymore. I've been to jail three times, the longest time for five months. I've had seven girlfriends and eleven cars. But I don't have to fight with Mattie, to prove myself to her every minute, like I'm doing with you now. That's why I want to be with her. What else?"

"Mattie's girlfriend number eight?"

"Number seven. Wife number two. What else?"

"The fact that there is an outstanding warrant for your arrest in Saskatoon?" Sara said.

He took a breath, then let it out. Sara held hers. "I borrowed that car from its rightful owner. It was a legitimate misunderstanding but she turned vindictive for no reason. I don't want to go to jail again. I don't deserve to."

Sara allowed herself no expression.

"You would, wouldn't you? I mean, you really would. I can see that. All right. I respect that, I do. You fight hard and you win."

She whispered, "Please leave."

He went upstairs. She knew this was the dangerous

time, the time when smashing sounds might begin. A few minutes later he came back down with a backpack. "Don't be scared," he said, when he saw her face.

He went into the TV room and a moment or two later came back, pursued by Mattie in tears. "I hate you!" she told Sara.

"No, Mattie," Robert said, "you don't."

Mattie had cried for days, had blamed Sara no matter how many times Sara tried to explain. Their appearance before the judge, Mattie prettily dressed and uncomprehending, was a gentle horror: everyone so understanding, so respectful of Mattie's dignity. The judge had spoken earnestly to Mattie, and Mattie had liked him, Sara could see. Mattie had become confused by her own emotions—loving Robert, loving Sara, loving the earnest judge with the funny big nose—and when they asked her if she wanted to say anything she had gotten tangled in her own thoughts, and blushed and shaken her head. So easy, Sara had thought, hating herself then.

Thus came the end of the privacy Sara had sought so fiercely and protected for so long. She sold the house— too big, too lavender-smelling—and moved Mattie into the second bedroom in her West End apartment, which had been her office. She would work from now on at a small desk in the hall. Mattie learned new bus routes, learned to manoeuvre in Sara's tiny galley kitchen, learned to operate the coin laundry machines in the basement, learned to manage two house keys—for the building, for the apartment door—instead of just one.

Sara learned more about Robert in the months after he had left their lives forever. She realized he had spent a lot of time with Mattie even before the marriage, enough to have remoulded Mattie to his own shape. He had been a good cook. "Too soft," Mattie said now of Sara's indifferently stir-fried vegetables, and she asked more than once when Sara was going to bake some muffins or roast a chicken. Robert had been a tidy man, and thrifty. Mattie counted the money in her beaded wallet every night now before she went to bed, and when she couldn't afford some treat she wanted, she said, "Never mind," instead of begging from Sara. She folded her laundry now and put it away, packing it into the drawers of her new, smaller dresser with thoughtful intensity, like she was packing for a sea voyage. Sara learned that Robert had been a man who liked to touch, casually, affectionately: a pat on the back, a kiss on the head, a head on her shoulder during the TV news on the sofa before bed. There was no one else from whom her sister could have learned this behaviour. There had never been anyone else at all.

Sara learned how Robert had been in bed. Late every night, after Sara had turned her light out—long after Mattie had closed her own door—Sara would feel her sister slip into her room, slip under the covers beside her, and press her body against Sara's until Sara put her arms around her. They would lie this way for a long time, until Mattie turned away, backing herself against Sara so that Sara would hold her that way, and then Mattie would sigh and busy her hands between her own legs. The doctor had assured Sara weeks ago that Mattie was healthy and her hymen intact. "You," Mattie would mumble after she was done, but Sara would only hold her. Every night after Mattie had fallen asleep Sara would promise herself to put an end to these intrusions: a gentle but firm talk, a lock on the door, a sharp, unequivocal word in the night.

But night rolled into day rolled into night and she said nothing, did nothing. She had taken the sun and the moon from Mattie, as the old words went; they would not come again. Skin on skin, and not to be alone: didn't she owe her this, at least, if her own love was true?

CHAPTER THREE

Fall 2015

Saskia Gilbert sat at her favourite carrel in the UBC library, surrounded by books. Her iPhone flashed a text from her father: *phone home*. She ignored it because it wasn't Jenny. Jenny would be working late, as usual, or out with friends. While Saskia was slogging her way through a graduate degree, her twin had charmed her way from an internship to a job with an interior design firm. She drove a hybrid and wore dresses and ate at the restaurants she helped style: the fusion sushi place, the retro-futuristic wine bar, the Brazilian-style churrascaria with the communal tables. Saskia had gone along with her to that one, only last week, and regretted it.

"Talk about your meat market," she'd mumbled into her wine.

"Would it kill you to talk to someone other than me?" Jenny accepted a skewer of blackened chicken from a passing waiter and flashed him her starlet's smile. The waiter winked. Saskia sighed. A woman across the table and a little ways down wore a delicate gold lamé camisole and white skinny jeans. The man next to her wore a plum-coloured suit that was either elegant and expensive or ridiculous. Jenny would tell her which. In her heavy-framed glasses, ponytail, and black hoodie, Saskia knew she looked like what she was: a depressed, penniless student who resembled her twin the way a raisin resembles a grape.

"Did you try that aromatherapy spray I gave you?" Jenny demanded. The man eyed Jenny, in her sky-blue silk shirt dress with her flawless makeup and French manicure and her designer tonic water. She'd left the chrome tube on Saskia's bedside table. Saskia guessed it cost more than she earned in a month of marking papers as a teaching assistant. That was Jenny, whiplashing so quickly from absurd generosity to bullying that sometimes it was hard to distinguish between them. The twins still lived in their parents' house, a massive Craftsman in Kerrisdale, roommates in the two-bedroom basement suite. As much as their lives had diverged, they weren't ready to leave each other.

"Not yet."

"We should go shopping. I'll give you a makeover."

"Why mess with perfection?"

"And there's this guy at work—"

"Jenny, stop."

"But you're so boring."

"I study French literature. You know, existentialism, *ennui*. Life is meaningless, *chérie*. It's an occupational hazard."

"You're twenty-seven. You should be dating."

"I should be finishing my thesis."

Jenny's phone shivered where it lay on the table, next to her plate. She glanced at it. "How's that going, anyway? Still stuck?"

Saskia was watching the woman in the gold top, who was sipping from a flute of Prosecco and flirting effortlessly with the man in the purple suit. "My advisor says it's unfocused. She says I need to start over."

"So start over."

"Maybe grad school's not for me. Maybe it's time to face the real world."

"Hallelujah."

"It's just that I know I'm getting closer." Saskia sipped her own wine, an eighteen-dollar glass she'd been nursing for too long because she couldn't afford a second. "I feel like I'm getting closer to understanding something about—" *You*, she wanted to say. *Us*. "Something about love. And pain. And—sadness."

Jenny's laugh was little bells, silver and gold. "Oh god,

Sass. Is this where you tell me you're depressed?" She tugged the string of Saskia's hoodie. "You're such a cliché." Her phone shivered again.

"Maybe you could turn that—"

"Hello?"

Saskia listened to Jenny flirt for a couple of minutes and then went to the washroom to kill time. When she came back, she found a note under her drink that said, *Got a better offer.*

Now, in the library, her own phone flashed again. *Phone home.*

Saskia set one book aside and reached for another. Her advisor, Madame Brossard, had been unequivocal that morning. No more half-finished papers and half-hearted ideas. She must stop reading and start writing. She was behind. Her scholarship was now in question.

Her phone's screen lit up with her parents' faces. Home was now phoning her. Her mother, vague with wine most afternoons; her father the workaholic QC with his bulldog ways. The big house could feel lonely and empty even when they were all there. Her father would work late in his home office. Her mother would drift around like a ghost, glass in hand, complaining of the headaches brought on by light, noise, music, or any kind of cheer. Jenny stayed out most nights; Saskia stayed in the basement.

Her parents' faces disappeared, replaced by a message indication. Almost immediately, their faces reappeared. They were calling again.

"Hello," Saskia whispered.

Her father. She could hear his voice booming, not at her, and then there he was in her ear. "Sassy. Are you there?"

Even his questions sounded like orders. "I'm here."

"Stop *whispering*, Sassy. We have an emergency. You're coming to the hospital right now."

"What—"

"St. Paul's. Now."

"Mom—?"

"Jenny."

She stared at the cover of the nearest book: Camus's *The Stranger*.

"Are you still there, Saskia?"

"I'm here."

"It was a car accident. Jenny's going to be fine."

But there was something in his voice, something choked. "Dad, are you crying?"

"She hasn't woken up yet. They think it's a concussion. *Now*, Sassy."

At some point in their conversation she had stopped whispering. A librarian was walking purposefully towards her, pointing at Saskia's phone and shaking her head.

"I'm on my way." Saskia stuffed the phone in her pocket, shrugged on her knapsack, and swept the books off the desk and into the arms of the surprised librarian. *The Stranger, The Myth of Sisyphus, Being and Nothingness, No Exit.*

"I won't be needing those," Saskia called over her shoulder as she ran.

Outside, late September's gold spangled the trees. The sky was that high, pale, honest blue of the last fine days before the fall rains set in. Saskia had parked her car in the lot near the law school. She shouldered her way past men and women her own age in suits and heels, people—as her father would have said—with *prospects.* She let her hair hang in her face and avoided eye contact when she crossed this part of campus. Her father had always assumed she'd follow him into law.

"You have the mind," he always told her, growing up. "You can article at my firm. I won't go easy on you, but I'll open doors. You'll go far."

And she had indeed gone far, as far away from his dream as she could. She shopped at thrift stores and studied dead French depressives. She drove a third-hand Corolla, not because her father wouldn't have bought her something better, but precisely because it was the car she could afford to pay for by herself out of a TA salary. She refused makeup, social occasions of any kind, the allowance her parents offered. She was, in her own way, just as willful as Jenny. They both hated to be told what to do.

"We'll go to Paris one day," her mother said weakly when she told them she was going to grad school to study comparative literature.

"You're wasting your talents, but suit yourself," her father had said. "I never would have thought your sister would turn out to be the success in the family."

Guilt rinsed through her when he said things like that. It was unfair to measure them against each other because they both knew Saskia would always win. Saskia the smart one, the sober one. The whole one.

And indeed it was Saskia he turned to when he needed someone to talk to about work, when their mother couldn't get out of bed, when Jenny maxed out her credit card for the tenth time, when he brought home a new Beethoven CD and needed someone to hear how beautiful it was. It was Saskia he was turning to now. *Pull yourself together.*

Ten deep breaths. She started the car, leaned over to the glove box, opened it, then snapped it shut.

She didn't think of Jenny while she navigated the early rush-hour traffic out of Point Grey, out of Kitsilano, across the Burrard Bridge and into downtown. She didn't think of Jenny as she circled St. Paul's, looking for street parking. She didn't think of Jenny even as she said her sister's name to the receptionist and was directed to the ICU. She didn't think of Jenny until she saw her parents in a room at the end of a corridor, standing by a green-curtained bed.

Her twin lay as though sleeping. Her head was bandaged and there was an IV drip taped to her arm. Her mouth was oddly slack under the respirator.

"Shh," her mother whispered. "She's tired."

Saskia hugged her. Her mother's eyes were far away.

Her father touched her mother's shoulder gently. "Mary, why don't you go take a seat in the waiting room for a minute? She's only allowed two visitors at a time. We'll give Sassy a chance, shall we?"

"Oh, yes," her mother said, and she wandered off.

"What did they give her?" Saskia asked.

"Ativan."

Saskia nodded.

"It's bad, Sassy." They hugged. She felt his shoulders heave once, and hugged him harder. When they separated, he pinched the bridge of his nose hard enough to leave a mark.

Saskia touched Jenny's hand, the one without the drip. Her skin was warm. She leaned down and kissed her cheek. Jenny didn't move.

"We spoke to the doctor about half an hour ago. They're running tests."

"What happened?"

"We're still trying to understand. The police claim she was speeding. She was T-boned at Oak and Forty-first."

Oakridge Centre, Saskia thought. Her sister loved to shop there.

"She wasn't wearing her seat belt and she went through a red light. They're saying her blood alcohol was point-one-seven."

They looked at each other. Jenny wasn't supposed to drink.

"I'm going to call Marcel." Marcel was a colleague of her father's, a partner in his firm. "He's the best in the business. He won't let the police roll over us."

"Surely it's not about rolling over us. She must have— I don't know. She's seemed so much better, lately. When we go out, she drinks tonic water."

"I called her office," Saskia's father said. "They thought she was on the North Shore with a client."

"Playing hooky to go shopping?" Saskia lowered her voice to a murmur. "I mean, it wouldn't be the first time."

A nurse gave the curtain a twitch, sending it down the rail. She was a tiny Filipina with a big smile. "How are we doing?" She seemed to be talking to Jenny, so neither Saskia nor her father answered. She checked Jenny quickly but thoroughly, then glanced at Saskia. "Your twin?"

Saskia blinked. "Most people can't tell."

"No, what are you talking about?" Saskia recognized the meaningless patter of a caregiver trying to set worried relatives at ease. "Like peas in a pod!"

"When is the doctor coming back?" Her father glanced at his watch. "I want another test for the blood alcohol. That first test was wrong. This has to be done immediately, and time-stamped. There are issues of liability here."

The nurse referred to her chart. "They've already taken a second sample. It's being tested now. The doctor's just waiting on all her results."

"Thank you," Saskia said, when her father didn't.

After the nurse left, Saskia's father asked her to check on her mother. "Get her to drink some water. The Ativan always makes her thirsty."

Saskia found her mother in the waiting room, chatting with a middle-aged man who seemed relieved when Saskia touched her shoulder, drawing her attention away from him. "Mom?"

"Hello, love." Her mother turned her empty-eyed smile on Saskia.

"Jenny's stable. Let's go down to the cafeteria. Are you hungry?"

They bought bottled water and coffee and apples and potato chips. Her mother used to bring her two girls to the hospital regularly, for twin studies when they were little and psychological testing later. Jenny always loved those visits, loved being the centre of attention. Saskia hated them.

"Why do I have to come?" she asked her mother once. "There's nothing wrong with me."

"Well, darling, I think that's the point." They looked over at fifteen-year-old Jenny, talking animatedly with the doctor, who was laughing. "You're the control."

After twenty minutes in the cafeteria, her mother said she was cold and wanted to go back upstairs. "Maybe Jenny's awake. We don't want to miss that."

They heard the shouting before they turned the corner into the long hall. A security guard in a black uniform rushed past them, followed by a man in a suit and wool overcoat trailing an expensive cologne. Saskia's mind caught up only belatedly with her eyes: Marcel.

"What's happening?" her mother asked.

Saskia ran after them. At Jenny's bedside, her father was berating the ER doctor while the security guard tried to put himself between them. "Incompetent son of a bitch," her father was booming. "I'll have you know that I'm—"

"Hugh," Marcel said loudly. "Let me handle this."

Saskia touched his elbow. "Dad. Daddy."

He turned to her with wild eyes.

"Mr. Gilbert," the doctor said. He seemed surprisingly calm. "I understand this is a profound shock. Our efforts here are not over. We are hiding nothing from you, and your daughter's care is our highest priority. But your daughter is not the only patient here. You *will* lower your voice in my hospital." This was delivered with the same steely calm Saskia had seen her father use to great effect in the courtroom.

"Sit down, Hugh." Marcel directed her father to one of the teal blue plastic chairs by Jenny's bed. Their mother sat beside him and pulled his face into her shoulder.

"Marcel Bouchard." Her father's colleague held out a hand to shake the doctor's. "I represent the family. This is the patient's sister, Saskia Gilbert." She, too, shook the doctor's cool hand. "Maybe you can fill us in."

While the security guard hovered at a discreet distance, watching her father, the doctor drew them a few steps down the corridor. He was older than he first looked. You noticed the tan and the lean body first, the tiredness and sprinkled grey hairs only up close. He addressed Saskia. "Your sister is in a coma. Like a deep sleep."

"Did you recheck her blood alcohol?" What her father would have asked.

The doctor hesitated. Then: "We did. There was no mistake. The alcohol may have contributed to the crash, but we think the coma was caused by a stroke. All the neurological tests haven't come back yet, though."

"She's twenty-seven. I thought old people had strokes."

"A stroke occurs when blood flow to the brain is interrupted." The three of them, as though of one mind, turned to look at Jenny. "There can be many causes. A clot, say, or in this case likely a head trauma from when she hit the steering wheel. Can you tell me about any medications she's on? Any drug use?"

Saskia looked at Marcel, who looked at the floor. "Jenny wasn't on any medications. She isn't supposed to drink or take drugs."

Marcel touched the doctor's elbow and led him a little further down the hall. Saskia went to Jenny's bedside, on the opposite side from her parents, and leaned down close. "I'm here," she whispered. "It's me. I know you're there."

Jenny didn't respond.

At around three that morning, Saskia drove her mother home. Her father insisted on staying with Jenny. The streets were deserted and all the lights were green. The drive, normally forty-five minutes from downtown, took twenty. The big Kerrisdale house was the only one on the street with lights on, and the front door was unlocked. Her parents had left in a panic when the call came from the hospital.

Saskia got her mother upstairs and into her robe. The master bedroom was a plush acre or so of thick, pale carpet, Japanese wallpaper with wading storks, fresh flowers, and hammered-silk curtains. Saskia helped her mother into her king-sized four-poster. Her hair was white-gold down on the gold raw-silk pillow. Jenny had styled this room for her sixtieth birthday, right down to the blue and white Chinese bowl on the bedside table to hold her mother's rings. Saskia placed a single Ativan in a trinket dish next to her vial of Seconal. By the time she got back from the bathroom with a glass of water, her mother was already asleep.

Saskia made her way downstairs, flicking off lights as she went. The door to the basement was through the kitchen, where she stopped briefly to make herself a tray of tea and crackers. Late as it was, she knew she wouldn't sleep.

The basement she and Jenny shared had two bedrooms, two bathrooms, a laundry room, a kitchen they rarely used, and a sitting area. This was Jenny's laboratory. She was always trying out different arrangements of furniture, painting this wall or that, bringing home fresh cushions and flea market antiques. Currently she was going with an Indian theme. The walls were spice-reds and browns, the footstool a brass elephant she'd found at a garage sale, and the couch was covered in an embroidered blue-and-orange sari she had repurposed as a throw.

Saskia put her tray on the elephant's back and dropped

onto the couch. The TV offered cop shows about serial killers, reality shows about serial killers, movies about serial killers, cooking shows, infomercials, and a black-and-white comedy from the forties featuring William Powell and Myrna Loy. Saskia sank her tired mind into that glamorous world of silks and furs and gangsters and fast talk.

"I'm a hero. I was shot twice in the *Tribune*."

"I read where you were shot five times in the tabloids."

"It's not true. He didn't come anywhere near my tabloids."

The movie went on while the windows slowly lightened: dawn. Saskia got up to pull the curtains. She needed the dark. She couldn't bring herself to go into Jenny's room, though, and pulled her door closed instead. She watched until the last credits had rolled, then turned the TV off and went to her own room to try for a couple of hours' sleep. She had promised her father she'd be back at the hospital by ten.

On her bedside table sat the chrome tube of aromatherapy spray Jenny had left for her. Saskia picked off the clear plastic sheathing with her fingernails and uncapped the tube.

Sandalwood—she recognized sandalwood. That was their mother's jewellery box, that smell. They used to take turns pushing their face into it and breathing deep.

Cinnamon, and something else: floral, but not sweet. Darkly intoxicating, what black roses would smell like.

"I had it custom mixed for you," Jenny had told her. "Everything I knew you'd love. Who knows you better than me? You can carry it around with you, take a whiff when you're feeling down. You'll be amazed how it re-arranges your brain, just one beautiful breath of it."

Anyone who didn't know Jenny would say it was a thoughtful gift. Certainly she had put thought into choosing something she knew Saskia would love, but only so she could use it as leverage later. *Tell Mum and Dad I came home late and left early,* when she stayed out all night. *I don't want to have dinner with them tonight, tell them I have to work late. If David* (or Liam or Ellie or Oliver or Rob) *calls, tell him I went to Seattle for the weekend. Cover for me. You owe me. I do things for you.*

Saskia wondered if Jenny was still able to smell. If she ever would again.

She capped the tube quickly and shoved it into a drawer, where its scent couldn't reach her.

Their days settled into a dreary pattern. They took turns at the hospital so Jenny would never be alone. Saskia and her father saw each other only in passing. The circumstances of the accident melted into inconsequence. The police interviewed Jenny's friends and work colleagues. They looked at her email and social media and text messages, and stated in their report that they had found nothing beyond the obvious: Jenny had a history of wildly erratic behaviour and a psychiatric diagnosis to match. She alone was to blame. The other driver, a young mother with toddlers in the back seat, was cleared of wrongdoing. None of them were harmed. There would be no court case.

Saskia asked her father if she might see Jenny's phone for herself. He was the one who had collected her sister's things from the police after they concluded their report—her bag, her phone, her clothes. They searched his office together, then his car, then his bedroom.

"I don't know, Sassy. I'm sure I got it all back. I just can't remember where I put it." He started to cry. "I keep having these gaps."

She hugged him. "We're all exhausted. It doesn't matter."

Saskia's mother sat at Jenny's side, sipping from her travel mug, getting in the nurses' way. Her father aged almost as Saskia watched him. He slumped rather than sat, and lost weight.

"How long do we keep this up?" he asked Saskia, as

they traded places, twelve days in, she to take his chair by the bedside, he to go home—if his experience was anything like hers—to takeout and insomnia.

"What do you mean?" But Saskia knew. They were waiting for Jenny to wake, but what if she never did? They couldn't do this for the rest of their lives. Her father was on stress leave from work, and she had simply stopped going to the University. But eventually their lives would have to resume.

Their father reached out to stroke Jenny's curls back from her forehead. The bandages had come off, but she now had a feeding tube and catheter as well as the IV and the respirator.

"I'm not ready to think about that," Saskia said.

Her father nodded.

Jenny looked so normal, so like herself. Sleeping Beauty. Someone had wiped the makeup from her face that first day, and though the nurses washed her hair, it went frizzy without styling products. Her mouth was just that little bit too slack. But still she looked tousled from a late Friday night and a hard sleep, about to open her eyes and smile and try to persuade Saskia to come out with her tonight, just this once.

After her father had left, Saskia reached in her purse for the chrome tube. Not the one Jenny had left for her, but its twin, the one she'd found on Jenny's bedside table last night, when she finally braved the door she'd closed on the first day. She'd sat on the floor, leaning against the open door, and tried to cry, hugging her sister's pillow, which smelled of her shampoo. Looking dully around the room, she'd spotted the tube.

Slowly she uncapped it and waved it near Jenny's face. It was different from Saskia's: lighter, sweeter. Pink flowers. It was her sister, utterly: sweet and pretty and charming and uncomplicated. A lie.

"Wake up," Saskia said. "Wake up, Jenny."

Nothing.

She waved the tube closer, brushing the tip of her sister's nose. She shook her shoulder. "You know this, Jenny. Come on, you recognize this. Wake up!"

"Miss?" an orderly said.

"Wake up! I know you can hear me!" Saskia was shaking her with both hands now.

"Miss."

She was escorted from the hospital by the orderly, who was kind but firm. Saskia was tired, she needed to go home, she was disturbing the other patients.

"Yeah, yeah, yeah." Saskia shrugged his hand from her shoulder.

She didn't go home. She got in her car and took ten deep breaths. Then she opened the glove box, clicked it closed, and drove to Oakridge Centre.

———

What had she been thinking? Drunk, unstrapped, blowing through a red light. What the hell had been going
through her head?

Saskia drove through that intersection and turned
right into the mall parking lot.

You don't start with clothes, she remembered Jenny saying. *Clothes come last. You have to fix yourself naked first.*

The salon, then, and the spa.

"That's going to take a while," the purple-streaked
receptionist at the salon said when Saskia listed everything she wanted done. "Cut and colour, facial, pedicure,
waxing—"

"The complete tune-up," Saskia said.

The receptionist looked blank.

Saskia touched her temple, the pain blossoming there.
"It's been a bad couple of weeks. I need you to fix me,
you know? Make things better. I mean, not everything,
obviously. But—I need to . . ."

The receptionist raised her eyebrows, waiting.

"I need to feel pretty." It was as close as she could get
to saying: *I need to see my sister again. Awake.*

The receptionist reached across the counter, removed
Saskia's glasses, and looked at her for a long moment.
"We can do that."

Once Saskia was in the chair, the blonde Japanese stylist pulled the elastic out of her hair. She lowered her head to Saskia's level and together they looked into the mirror. "Is this natural?" She fingered a curl.

"Yeah. I never really know what to do with it, though."

"People pay a lot of money for hair like this. Do you always wear it in a ponytail?"

"Pretty much."

The stylist looked unimpressed. "And what are we doing today? Let me guess. A trim, but long enough so you can—"

"Put it back in a ponytail," Saskia finished for her.

"So, we're going to wash it first," the stylist said. "Then I'm going to talk you out of that."

The stylist led her to the sink. "I need you to relax, okay? Relax your neck and your head. And your shoulders."

Gush of warm water, lather of orange-smelling suds, and the girl's strong fingers working her scalp. All Saskia could think of was Jenny. Did she feel it when the nurses washed her hair? Could she feel the warm water, smell the lather, feel like a pleasured animal under the scalp massage? How much attention had Saskia herself ever paid to these things? She went to Kwik Kuts. Pleasure had never been part of the equation, never been a part of what she was paying for.

She closed her eyes and inhaled the fragrance of the shampoo, and thought about where fragrance went in your body: how it started in the nose, then filled the head, then travelled somehow to the lungs, the finger-tips, the—she hesitated, looking for the right word—the privates. Everything warmed and swelled and relaxed, just from the smell.

Privates? She could hear Jenny laughing. *That's what you call them? Like soldiers?*

Genitalia?

Peals of little silver bells.

Chrysanthemum, Saskia thought, remembering a French novel she had read. I feel it in my chrysanthe-mum. She imagined Jenny howling with laughter, col-lapsing on the sofa and snorting until her stomach ached.

The stylist wrapped her hair in a warm towel and led her back to the chair by the mirror. "A little colour?"

Saskia had never coloured her hair in her life. She had no grey, so what was the point?

"We'll just look, for fun." The stylist handed her a card like a large menu with tiny looped clips of coloured hair taped next to even tinier numbers. The stylist tapped a jade-green fingernail against one. "I like this for you."

"Seriously?" Saskia glanced at herself in the mirror. She couldn't picture it.

"And we need to get rid of some of this length. It's too

heavy. It's pulling the curls straight so you can't even see them. And this frizz at the ends? This is damage. I need to get rid of all this."

Saskia handed her back the menu. "Tell you what. You do it, okay? I trust you. Just—do what you think will work. You're the boss."

"What the fuck are you playing at?" her father said. "Your sister's in a coma and you go to the hairdresser? This is why you're late? We thought something happened to you."

Her mother was pale with shock. "I thought you were Jenny, walking through the door," she whispered. "I thought Jenny had come home."

"I'm sorry," Saskia said. "I didn't mean to—I didn't realize. I just needed a change."

"A *change*?" A vein pulsed in her father's forehead.

"I'm sorry," Saskia whispered.

They had planned a rare supper together at home. It had been almost three weeks since the accident, and they were all worn out by keeping vigil at Jenny's bedside twenty-four hours a day. Her father had asked her mother to cook a meal, had asked Saskia to be home for six o'clock. Saskia knew a talk was coming, *the* talk. They had to get on with their lives. He had to go back to work.

Saskia had to go back to school. Decisions would have to be made.

Had Saskia written "Decisions would have to be made" in a paper, Madame Brossard would have circled it with her red pen. "In grammar, this is called the passive voice," she would say. "We cannot tell who is making these decisions. It is vague, it avoids accountability. Politicians love the passive voice, yes? French academics, not so much. Again, please."

They would have to make decisions: her father, her mother, Saskia. They would have to decide whether to keep hoping for Jenny's recovery or to wall themselves off from that hope and try to get on with their lives.

When the stylist was done, Saskia had put her glasses back on and looked in the mirror. Jenny looked back: sleek, sultry, polished. Her brows tweezed, her skin pink, her lips cherry, her hair darker and glossier and curlier, her nails brightened with the French tips Jenny favoured. The tiny extra weight of the manicure on her fingertips distracted her for days.

Cutting her hair was a betrayal.

"If I wear my hair down, I'm going to look like Jenny," she said now. "I mean, obviously. We're twins. I'm sorry if I scared you."

"You're sorry." Her father shook his head.

Her mother couldn't look away. Even as she walked

towards the kitchen, her eyes slid sideways, watching Saskia as though she were a dangerous dog.

"Smells good," Saskia said.

"It's ready. We might as well eat."

They sat at the table while her mother served lasagna and salad. Her father poured wine for himself and Saskia.

"Are you wearing makeup?" her father demanded.

"Just a little."

"It's uncanny." His voice had gone gruff. Saskia recognized the tone that came when his anger was down to the embers, almost out.

"You look lovely." Her mother was clearly trying to rally.

"Would it be better if I took off the makeup?"

"Yes," both her parents said.

When she came back to the table, face washed, her parents broke off their whispered conversation.

"That's a new dress," her mother said.

"You hate it."

"No. It's different for you, that's all. But you need new clothes. It's time you started dressing like a grown-up. I think I will have that glass of wine, thank you, darling."

Her father complied. Saskia saw he was too tired to fight. She looked down at her lap so she wouldn't have to see her mother's thirst. She smoothed her napkin over the cool silk. After the salon she had meant to drive home, she really had, but she had instead gone into a store she recognized from the bags Jenny would bring home after a day's shopping. One of Jenny's favourites. At first she was intimidated by the polished wood floor, the quiet after the Muzak of the mall, and the expensive coats and dresses softly spot-lit, displayed like museum pieces. But then the saleslady, a woman her mother's age, smiled warmly and came around the counter to greet her. "Welcome back. We haven't seen you in a while."

After only the slightest hesitation: "I've been sick."

"I've saved some pieces for you."

In the change room Saskia stripped, leaving her black T-shirt and grey hoodie and jeans in a morose pile on the floor. The first dress was a simple grey jersey tunic with silver embroidery along the hem. "Wear it with tights and boots and that blue leather jacket of yours," the saleslady said when she stepped through the curtain. The second was a green shirt dress, the kind where Saskia would do up four buttons and Jenny would do up three. Today, Saskia did up three. The third dress was a blue silk shift, so pale at the shoulders it was almost white, deepening shade by shade through an ombré dye to indigo at the hem.

Jenny couldn't look away from the mirrors. "I'll wear this one home."

"I should think so," the saleslady said.

The other two dresses and her university clothes went into the glossy bag with the silk cord handles and the familiar logo. Saskia paid more than she had for last term's tuition.

"Do me a favour, honey," the saleslady said before she left. Saskia nodded. "Your shoes."

They both looked down. Under the blue silk, Saskia was wearing Doc Martens.

Two pairs of heels, three scarves, and a bracelet later, Saskia went home.

"I've been thinking." Saskia took some more salad. "I've been thinking about what Jenny would want."

Her parents were childlike, listening. They looked so, so tired.

"She'd want us to—to *live*. I mean, really to live. To enjoy life. Like she did. She wouldn't want us to—I don't know how to say it. To shut down."

Her mother stared into her wine.

"What are you suggesting?" her father said.

Saskia didn't know what she was suggesting. She knew that as she crossed the parking lot to her car after she came out of the mall, a man had taken one look at her and tripped over his own feet. Not something that had ever happened to Saskia.

Thank you, Jenny.

You're welcome, my little chrysanthemum.

In the kitchen, the phone rang.

"That'll be the office," her father said. "Marcel's held the fort as long as he can, but some of my files are getting urgent."

Her mother reached for his hand, then Saskia's. Saskia reached for her father's other hand to close the circle. They sat at the table, listening to the phone ring.

"I'll get it," her mother said finally.

Saskia and her father let go of her hands, but continued to hold each other's. They listened to her mother walk to the kitchen, pick up the receiver, and say her quiet hello.

"She's drinking again," her father said. "Well, I mean, she was before all this. Started again about a year ago."

Saskia nodded.

"I've been looking at clinics." He took her hand in both his, then spread her fingers to study her nails. He was carefully avoiding her eyes. "Detox. I think it might be time."

Saskia nodded again. "That's a really good idea, Daddy. I'll help, any way I can."

"You're not going off the rails on me, are you?" He touched her nails gently, one by one, as though brushing away invisible dust. "Trying to turn yourself into your sister? I can hardly look at you."

"I don't want to be her," Saskia said slowly. "But I want to—live for her. Look at me, Daddy. It's me. It's Saskia. I'm still here."

Slowly he raised his eyes to hers.

"I know," he said finally. "I'll always know my Sassy."

"Hugh!" their mother shouted.

"Damn that Marcel." Her father let go of her hand.

Their mother appeared in the doorway. "Get your coats. Both of you." The colour in her cheeks was high and her eyes were blazing. "Now, now! Where are the car keys?"

"Mom?"

"Mary. Mary, calm down."

"I will not calm down." Her mother's face flowered into an incredulous smile. "That was the hospital. Jenny opened her eyes."

Jenny's hospital room was filled with white coats, which parted to let the family approach the bedside. Their mother cried out softly, and her father surged forward to take Jenny's hand. She hadn't moved, but her eyes were open. She seemed to see their father, but Saskia couldn't tell if she recognized him. He stroked Jenny's hair back from her forehead and leaned down to kiss her cheek. Their mother kissed her also, and then they moved aside for Saskia.

"Hi." Saskia leaned down for her own kiss. "Welcome back."

Jenny blinked. Her eyes moved—she was looking around the room—but there was no recognition, no light or spark there.

"Don't be scared," Saskia said.

Jenny looked at her.

"She may not recognize you right now." A voice behind them; the family turned to this new authority. He shook each of their hands in turn. "Dr. Zhang, neurology. Opening her eyes is a great sign. We're hopeful she'll start to put things together over the next few weeks."

"Weeks?" their mother said.

"In situations like this, nothing happens overnight." This doctor looked not much older than Saskia. "Patients coming out of a coma usually experience a period of disorientation. It's like waking up really slowly, and you're not sure what's still a dream and what's real."

"Can she move?" Saskia asked.

The doctor shook his head before she'd even finished the sentence. "But if she wakes up all the way, physiotherapy will start."

"If?" their father said.

"Well, she could close her eyes again." Doctor Zhang approached Jenny's bedside. "I know in this moment it's hard, but you have to manage your hopes. Sometimes the movement of the eyes is just a biological function, like a reflex. But her other vital signs are promising." He spoke to Jenny directly. "We haven't given up on you, not by a long shot, gorgeous."

Jenny blinked.

"What do we do now?" Saskia asked.

"Well, we wait. And if she does close her eyes again, she might just be sleeping normally. Don't expect, and don't despair."

While their father shook the doctor's hand, Saskia leaned close to her sister. "I'll come every day."

The next morning, for the first time in a month, Saskia got in her car and drove to the University. Her parents had spent the night at the hospital, and she had promised to relieve them after lunch. She was wearing the new grey dress and Jenny's blue leather jacket.

September's gold had yielded to raw October. The leaves were coming down, and the weather had turned drizzly. Still, Saskia felt calm and focused in a way she hadn't since the accident.

On 10th Avenue, just before the University gates, Saskia stopped at a patisserie for breakfast. Usually she had tea and toast at home, but this morning she wanted to celebrate. She took her almond croissant and café au lait to a table. Normally she would have pulled out a book or her laptop and eaten without noticing, putting the necessary calories into herself while she worked. This morning she forced herself to notice the sensations of eating: the shattering crispness of the croissant and the smoky, chocolaty taste of the coffee. Good coffee had many flavours in it, like wine—how had she never noticed this before?

"Saskia?"

She looked up from the tiny, sensual feast of her breakfast. It was Madame Brossard, who hesitated by her table with her own coffee and croissant.

"Is that you?"

Saskia touched her hair. "I got it cut."

She made room at the table and gestured for her advisor to join her.

"You went missing," Madame said reprovingly. "I almost sent out a search party."

Saskia explained that her sister had been in an accident and she had spent the last couple of weeks at the hospital. Madame's face hardened a little even as she reached for Saskia's hand to give it a squeeze. It was a kind of French stoicism Saskia had noticed before, a sternness in the face of emotion.

"I will pray for her," Madame said.

They talked then, with an intimacy that had never

existed between them before. Madame described her father's lingering death, the year before, from stomach cancer. She knew the hospital well. Saskia thought, but did not remark, that she had taken classes with Madame all last year and never suspected a thing. Saskia, in turn, confessed her profound unhappiness with her studies, her inability to articulate what she felt most passionate about, and the frustration of this.

"I thought you were lazy," Madame said.

"I read and write and nothing comes together." Saskia fiddled with her new bracelet, a simple silver chain. "I feel more and more like the books I've been reading aren't the right ones. Camus, Sartre—I don't know if I'm interested in despair or meaninglessness anymore. Is that awful?"

Madame laughed, a surprisingly low, sexy laugh, enhanced (Saskia guessed) by years of cigarettes. "Two-thirds of my graduate students want to read Camus. It is a stage they have to grow out of. Like, when you are a parent, the diapers."

"That's a little harsh."

"Me, I adore Camus. But true scholarship isn't just admiration. One must be willing to turn the critical eye. Tell me, what perplexes you most in life?"

"I'm sorry?"

"Always I have thought that is an odd expression in

English. You mean to say *I don't understand,* but instead you say *I'm sorry.* There is no shame in ignorance. No reason to apologize. What perplexes you? What do you not understand, such that you are driven to read so many books?"

"Loneliness," Saskia said without thinking.

Madame clapped her hands. "*Bravo.* Now we are getting somewhere. You have made some changes to yourself. In the last few days, I think. Since I have last seen you. Since your sister's accident, *non?*"

"Oui." Saskia gave her a tiny, wry smile.

"*Alors.* Your sister's condition leads you to thoughts of the body, pleasure, sensuality. I see your hair, your clothes, I watched you eat your croissant before I came over. Loneliness sends you into your body instead of your brain, now, and this is new for you, I think."

"Very new," Saskia admitted.

"I was once the mistress of an older man." Madame rested her chin in her hand and Saskia saw in her face the ghost of a much younger woman. "In Paris. He was an intellectual, very famous. If I said his name to you, you would know it. Academically, it was the most fruitful period of my life. Incredibly productive. We fought about everything, like a pair of lobsters. After, I utterly changed the course of my thesis."

"Because of him?"

"Because of me." Madame tapped a fingernail on the tabletop. "I am remembering a paper you wrote me two years ago, while you were still an undergraduate. A paper on Laclos. Do you remember it? You still have a copy?"

Saskia nodded.

"You will give it to Professor Taillac. He, too, is interested in loneliness. He will be interested in meeting with you."

When she got to Jenny's bedside that afternoon, her parents told her that Jenny had slept for a while, then opened her eyes again. They had tried to get her to communicate by blinking—one for yes, two for no—but so far she didn't seem to understand.

"Brain damage is a real possibility," their father said.

"Are you wearing Jenny's jacket?" their mother said.

"She gave it to me," Saskia said.

After they left, Saskia sat in the teal chair. "My thesis advisor wants to drop me. She wants me to go to Taillac. You remember I told you about him?"

Jenny didn't move.

"Because of an undergrad paper I wrote after we rented *Les Liaisons dangereuses.* I'm so screwed."

Jenny blinked.

"She thinks I need to abandon existentialism altogether. She thinks I should focus on the erotics of loneliness."

Jenny blinked.

"Erotica, sure. Taillac? Stab me in the eye with a fork." Saskia dug in her purse and produced the chrome tube. "Look what I brought you." She uncapped it and waved it under her sister's nose. Jenny closed her eyes, then opened them. She blinked.

"I miss you," Saskia said.

Jenny blinked again.

"Are you doing that on purpose?"

Jenny blinked.

Saskia felt the breath go out of her. "You can hear me?"

Jenny blinked.

"Can I have your jacket?"

Jenny blinked twice. Saskia laughed so hard the nurses came running.

In the days that followed, they learned—finally—the true nature of Jenny's condition. She was "locked in"; that was the medical term. Her brain, her mind, her consciousness, her soul, whatever you wanted to call it, was intact. But because of the damage to her brain stem sustained in the accident, she couldn't speak, eat, move, or do anything by herself. She could communicate only by blinking, a process so painfully slow that Saskia got used to seeing tears creep down Jenny's cheeks as she struggled to make herself understood. A feeding tube pumped nourishment directly into her stomach and a ventilator helped her breathe. She drooled constantly. Her lips and chin became chapped and sore.

One day a hospital speech therapist came by and taught the family a code to make communication easier. The therapist had rearranged the letters of the alphabet in the order they most commonly appeared in English: E-T-A-O-N-R-I-S-H-D and so on. Now Jenny could spell out words. They would read the code to her, slowly, until she blinked at a letter. They would write that letter down, and start again.

The first word Jenny spelled was *love*. The second was *pain*.

CHAPTER FOUR

At first, Saskia's conversations with Jenny were frustrating. She had to learn not to try to finish words for her sister, to distinguish purposeful blinks from eye-clearing blinks, not to rush through the alphabet, not to ask her too many questions at once. Some days Jenny refused to cooperate, and in the hallways the nurses would whisper to her that Jenny was depressed. On those days, Saskia would hold up books and magazines until Jenny blinked her consent, and then she would read to her. They'd leaf through *Vogue* together and *The New Yorker*—Jenny's subscriptions—and Saskia brought in travel guides to Italy, Jenny's favourite country. She was well aware that to the nurses this looked like a kind of cruelty, but Jenny had told her once—blinked at her—that her imagination was all she had now, and when she had no visitors she would travel in her mind.

Saskia asked what she remembered about the accident; nothing, Jenny claimed. It was hard at the best of times to tell when Jenny was lying. Impossible, now.

Their father had gone back to work the way a pit bull goes back to a mailman's leg—grim, ferocious, unrelenting, joyless. He used work, now that Jenny's condition appeared fixed, to avoid the hospital. Their mother continued to visit regularly, but was refusing rehab for herself. She would sit at Jenny's bedside, but couldn't get the hang of the alphabet code and would only read children's books to her, because she didn't want to "upset" Jenny. Most often she would sit holding Jenny's hand and staring into space, sipping from her travel mug, until it was time to take a taxi home. She no longer drove.

On Jenny's orders, Saskia resumed her classes. *You need something else to do,* Jenny said. *It was hard enough babysitting you when I wasn't like this.* That had been a bad day: Jenny depressed and cruel, Saskia crying in the hospital washroom. But Saskia quickly realized the time apart was good for them both. School was different now. Saskia wore her sister's clothes, spent less time in the library, and even went on a date.

Saskia told Jenny about how she had met Joel in seminar—he was a recently arrived transfer student from Moncton—and how after their second class they had made their ways, separately, to a campus café, where Saskia was emboldened to approach him by the prospect of entertaining Jenny with the story later. How long his eyelashes were, and how he had stuttered, actually stuttered, when he asked her to go to a movie with him.

"A matinee." Saskia smiled wryly. She could almost hear Jenny's voice: *Ah, matinees. The quickest way to a girl's chrysanthemum.*

"I think I might actually have to make the first move," Saskia said.

It was one of Jenny's better days. Saskia held up the code board and eventually Jenny spelled out, *$10 no kiss xmas.*

"You're on." Saskia pulled a ten from her purse and tucked it into the book they'd been reading, for a bookmark. She took a tissue and wiped Jenny's mouth, then took up the board again.

Bracelet.

Saskia held up her arm to show her—a jade bangle. "Do you like it?"

Jenny blinked. Saskia took it off and clasped it around Jenny's wrist. Now Jenny owed her.

"I don't think I've ever seen you wear the same thing twice," Joel said to her, the second time they went out. The matinee, a documentary about a little-known jazz musician, had led to this second date, beer and burgers at a pub just off campus. Joel, endearingly, had dressed up, in a black shirt, black sweater, and brown cords. Saskia wore jeans and a black silk top artfully slashed with deep, narrow *v*'s between the breasts, over one shoulder, down her spine. Over this she wore Jenny's softest, demurest pink cardigan, as well as knee-high black patent-leather boots.

"A lot of what I wear is my sister's," she admitted.

Joel smiled. "I have sisters. I've seen them fight over clothes. She doesn't mind, your sister?"

Saskia looked at her lap.

"Did I say something wrong?"

She looked up again and saw that Joel looked stricken. This was the moment, the cusp. She could be honest with him, or she could pretend, the way she'd been pretending with everyone else who looked at her and saw her sister, and she hadn't set them straight.

"Hey." He reached across the table, tentatively, and touched her hand. "Are you crying?"

"Little bit."

He gave her his napkin, and didn't let go of her hand while she dabbed her eyes and nose. When she was able to speak again, she told him the whole story.

"My god." He shook his head, again and again. "Saskia, my god. I had no idea."

"It's been five weeks. We're still figuring out how to—I

don't even know what. How to carry on, I guess. My parents aren't doing too well. And I'm wearing my sister's clothes, so whatever that says about me—"

"That says you love her."

Saskia felt a flash of weary irritation. She had spent her entire life being told how close she and Jenny were, how much they loved each other, how she was Jenny's rock. The truth was so much more complicated than that. *Of course* she and Jenny were closer to each other than anyone else. That closeness didn't shield her from Jenny's manipulations, her cruelty. *Of course* Saskia loved Jenny. That didn't mean she wasn't also frightened of her, and frightened for her, even before the accident. Jenny was the kind of person who could fly away or go up in flames at any moment. It was exhausting to be her counterweight, her rock, her extinguisher, her control. Not to know—when she didn't come home—whether that meant an all-nighter at work, or a date, or an impetuous trip to San Francisco because Jenny had been driving to the dentist and got distracted by the signs pointing to the airport.

"I hated her," Saskia said. "Sometimes. We always knew something was wrong, but the doctors wouldn't diagnose her until she was an adult. They said she might outgrow her symptoms. She never cared about other people, about pleasing them or hurting them. She stole both my high school boyfriends just because she could. She could be violent when we were little, but that faded away."

Joel shook his head.

"She's no danger to anyone but herself. She's always had trouble controlling her impulses, trouble staying with one thing—one job, one relationship. She doesn't much care about anyone's feelings but her own. But she'd been doing really well, keeping her appointments with the therapist and holding a job. She was even talking about moving out of our parents' house, getting an apartment somewhere. Before the accident."

Joel shook his head. "I don't know what to say."

No one ever knew what to say; she was used to that too. "You could tell me about *your* sisters."

They talked for another hour, Joel idly stroking her fingers. Outside, though, he didn't try to hold her hand. They got in Saskia's car and she offered to drop him anywhere he wanted to go.

"Oh, anywhere on Granville. I can grab a bus home from there."

She reached across him, opened the glove box, clicked it closed, and started the engine.

"Why do you do that? That thing with the glove box."

"Nervous habit, I guess."

"Are you worried it's going to fall open while you're driving?"

"No." Saskia rolled her window down, but didn't pull out of their parking spot. "It's a trick my dad taught me, okay? To control your emotions. You put what you're feeling in a box, and you close it firmly. Then you can function."

Joel laughed. "You know that's pretty neurotic, right?"

"Yeah, I know."

While she drove to Granville, they planned their next date, a bike ride along the beach the following weekend. At the bus stop, he leaned over and kissed the top of her head, then blushed pink and hopped out of the car before she could respond.

Professor Taillac was an asshole.

"Cécile is giving me her dregs again." He looked over Saskia's plan of study. "I'm not interested in this existentialist shit."

"Neither am I," Saskia said. Taillac raised his eyebrows. "I need to start over."

Taillac might have been sixty, but he wore it like forty-five. He had the decaying looks of a fading movie star, and a reputation for sleeping with his students. Saskia knew she had nothing to fear from him, though: he liked them dumb and pretty. To him, Saskia was work, only work.

"I'm interested in the intersection of solitude and

physical sensation in literature, particularly eighteenth-century literature. Prévost, Laclos, writers like that."

He stared at her for a long time across his big oak desk. She forced herself to meet his gaze.

"Well, what?" he said finally. "Go write me a paper or something. I'm interested in oysters for lunch. That doesn't give us anything to talk about right now, either."

When Saskia arrived at the hospital the next day, a man she'd never seen before was sitting at Jenny's bedside with the code board. He wore light blue hospital scrubs.

"You must be Saskia." He rose and held out his hand. "Jenny's told me about you."

Saskia channelled Professor Taillac, and raised her eyebrows.

"I'm her speech therapist. I've been assigned her case. Mostly we're working on swallowing at the moment. We tried a little yoghurt this morning and that didn't go so well, did it? But we'll keep trying. You're twins?"

"Hi," Saskia said to Jenny. "Sorry I'm late. I had a meeting with Taillac. Yes, twins." She turned to the speech therapist. She saw his eyes flicker across Jenny's monitors, then back to her. "She has a feeding tube."

"She told me she wanted pudding."

Saskia looked at Jenny, who blinked once. Pudding had been her favourite dessert when she was little.

"Typically, when we're reintroducing solids, we start with yoghurt and work our way up from there. Even if she still gets the bulk of her nourishment from the tube, it's nice to taste a bit of something."

When the speech therapist had left, Saskia said, "You've made a friend."

Jealous?

"Surprised."

He's all right. Doesn't talk down to me.

"I'm sorry the yoghurt didn't work out."

Next time.

Professor Taillac was an asshole. "I've read this paper a dozen times," he said at their next meeting, tossing it across the desk. Unlike Madame Brossard's barbed wire overlay of red ink, he had written nothing. "Boring," he added, in case she'd missed his point. "Next you'll be writing about *Babette's Feast*. Do you know the difference between sensuality and pornography?"

Saskia, furious, inclined her head with elaborate courtliness. *Do tell?*

"Expand your reading. Try again."

"He wants me to write a paper on pornography," she told Jenny. "He says I'm boring."

Jenny blinked twice, *no*. She seemed tired today.

"Well, my work. I have no idea what he thinks of *me*." Saskia wiped Jenny's mouth, adjusted her blanket. "I guess some people would say I'm lucky. I have to read porn for school. Every student's dream, no?"

Jenny closed her eyes.

"I'm sorry. All I do is talk about me. Did the speech therapist come back? Did you try the yoghurt again?"

But Jenny's eyes stayed closed.

French pornography. Where to start? Saskia decided on Pauline Réage's *Story of O* from 1954. Definitely not eighteenth century, but linked to de Sade—the author's lover, the intended audience for the book, admired de Sade and told the author he didn't believe a woman could write like that. She had accepted the challenge.

"I don't know," she told Joel. "I don't know what to say. I don't find it sexy. It bores me, actually. But, then, so did *Lolita*."

"That's because you're a normal, healthy, well-adjusted person." Joel was less interested in literature than foreign policy, and wanted to go into journalism. French linguistics class was their intersection. "Your whole thesis confuses me, if I'm being honest. How is pornography about solitude?"

"It's a metaphor," Saskia began.

"How's your sister?"

"Changing the subject."

Joel shrugged.

"Okay, I guess. I don't know. The last couple of visits she seemed to tire a little faster than usual. Didn't want to communicate much."

Joel hesitated. "I'd like to meet her sometime. If that's not—if your family—"

Saskia leaned across the table and kissed him, so quickly that she half missed his mouth and caught his cheek, sandpapery with a day's growth of stubble. He looked down at the table and then up at her, pleased, blushing again.

In the back of Saskia's mind, O sat leashed, knees wide, in her owl mask. *Go away,* Saskia thought at her, but of course she wouldn't.

She came home to find a dark sedan with a discreet emergency light in the rear window parked in the driveway. Inside, two plain-clothes cops sat at the dining table with her mother, who was drinking frankly, for once, with a proper wineglass and an almost empty bottle open on the sideboard. The cops had full glasses of water. They looked up when Saskia came in.

"Oh, it's not Hugh." Her mother smiled hazily at Saskia. "Well, he'll be home next."

The cops were an older woman and a younger man. Saskia could see their caution.

"Jenny?" Saskia said.

"She's fine." The female cop stood to shake Saskia's hand. "Your mother—we thought we might wait for Mr. Gilbert."

"Mom, why don't you let me take care of this?" Obediently her mother rose from her chair and let Saskia lead her upstairs to her bedroom.

"You're tired today," Saskia lied as she steered her to her bed. "You should rest a bit. Dad and I will take care of everything."

Her mother's eyes were already closed. She would sleep for several hours, now, and wake deep in the night with a headache, calling her hangover insomnia.

Downstairs, Saskia took her mother's place across the table from the cops. "Jenny," she repeated. It wasn't a question this time.

"We understand your father will be home shortly?" The younger cop, the man, spoke this time.

"Is this about Jenny's accident?" Saskia asked the woman cop.

They heard the front door and all three stood up. Saskia's father appeared, looking frightened and exhausted. His eyes found Saskia's face.

"Mom's upstairs, lying down," she said quickly. "Jenny's the same."

"What is this?" her father asked the male cop.

"Please." The female cop gestured to a chair, Saskia's chair as it happened. She was sitting in his usual place. "We're here to fill you in on something that occurred earlier this evening at the hospital. Your daughter is unharmed. We're not even sure how much she's aware of."

As she was speaking, Saskia's father gestured to the sideboard. Saskia got up and found him a pad of paper in a drawer, and he took a pen from his shirt pocket. The female cop waited while he turned to a clean page. "Please," he said curtly, pen poised.

There was actually very little to tell. At 4:45 p.m., a nurse performing a routine check on the ward found a man in Saskia's room. She called hospital security, who tried to apprehend the man on his way out of the building, but he ran. By the time the police got there, he was gone.

"Gone," her father repeated. He looked up from his notes.

"He was masturbating," the female cop said. "He had pulled the bedclothes down and exposed your daughter's breasts. We don't believe he assaulted her otherwise."

In the days that followed, her father made decision after decision. Too quickly; too quickly for any of them to fully absorb. He worked in a fever, a rage. He quit his job to focus exclusively on the daughter he'd neglected, the daughter he'd failed. He brought a lawsuit against the hospital. He had the smaller sitting room, next to his home office, fitted with a bed and monitors. He arranged for twenty-four-hour nursing care and booked the hospital transfer.

"Talk him out of it," Dr. Zhang told Saskia bluntly.

But there was no talking him out of it. He believed only in himself, now, and thought he could protect Jenny, heal Jenny, through sheer force of will.

"Talk him out of it," Marcel Bouchard begged Saskia. But she didn't try.

That first night, after the appalling scene with the police officers, her father had asked her to go to Jenny.

"Come with me, Daddy," she had said, but he could not. He was ashamed, he was crying, but he could not, just then, look at his little girl. Saskia felt the pressure of the great bubble of academic knowledge that filled her brain, that informed her understanding of her father. Historical context, literary examples, even deep-seated religious influences warped and wefted in her head to explain his revulsion. Academically, rationally, she could read him. He blamed Jenny, knowing she was blameless.

He believed Jenny changed, though she lay changeless in her hospital bed. The child/woman, virgin/whore, daughter/stranger. He was not very original, her father. All this wove itself in her head on the cab ride to the hospital. She had no idea, herself, what to expect from her sister.

Dr. Zhang met her in the hallway outside the room where a security guard sat in a plastic chair. The nurses watched from a distance. When she went in, Jenny's eyes stayed closed. Saskia hugged her and kissed her smooth, warm cheek. Dr. Zhang said something about the hospital reviewing its protocols.

"Did she tell you anything?" Saskia asked.

"She's been sleeping. We think she might have slept through the whole thing."

"She's not sleeping," Saskia said softly.

When Dr. Zhang left the room, Jenny opened her eyes. "Are you all right?" Saskia asked.

Jenny blinked once. She blinked twice. She closed her eyes.

"Talk him out of it," her mother whispered, just once. Her big blue eyes swimming, pleading. Five days before the transfer, a week after the incident, her father was downstairs bullying the movers who were setting up

Jenny's room. Her mother lay in bed, painfully sober and self-aware. "I can't cope. I'm useless."

"Jenny is stable. Go back to Shelby for a few weeks. Come home when you're ready. It was so good for you last time." Shelby was a private clinic outside of Kelowna, discreet and expensive. Every few years her mother went there for a month and returned pinker and plumper and changed forever.

Jenny came home one rainy afternoon in November. The sky was charcoal and the streetlights were butter. The paramedics eased her stretcher out of the van and up the front steps and into the room her father had prepared. Saskia and her father stayed back, letting them do their work. Saskia had dropped her mother at the airport the day before. The flight to Kelowna took less than an hour, and she would be met at the gate by an attendant from Shelby, who would see to her bags and everything else. Her mother would be fine.

When the paramedics left, the wise old owl of a night nurse checked the monitors, touching each one, and straightened the bedclothes. Then she took her seat in the chair next to the bed and pulled out some knitting. Saskia went around the house closing the blinds and turning on lights. Her father poured himself a cranberry soda and sat in his office, next to Jenny's room, reading a magazine. Jenny slept.

The second-to-last time Jenny opened her eyes, it was to meet Joel. Saskia had not mentioned the incident to him, had only told him they thought Jenny would be more comfortable at home. After class they got in her car. Saskia watched Joel take in the neighbourhood, old Vancouver money, and the mansion her family called home. She watched him not remark on her father's Jaguar when she parked her shitty Corolla next to it, not remark on their half-acre or so of kitchen, all brushed steel and teak (she had brought him in the back way, as was her habit, through what her father only half-jokingly called the servants' entrance), not remark on the art or the rugs or the sheer scope of the place.

"Jenny, this is Joel," Saskia said. "I've told you about him."

The nurse had stepped out to give them some privacy, abandoning her knitting in the chair. Jenny opened her eyes.

"It's so nice to meet you," Joel said. "Saskia's told me so much about you."

They pulled chairs up next to the bed and made awkward small talk for the next fifteen minutes or so, not bothering with the board. Joel made an effort to speak directly to Jenny, though she was uncommunicative. She slept almost all the time now, but Doctor Zhang had warned them to expect this after the stress of the move. He hoped she would become communicative again once she had adjusted.

Saskia took Joel to meet her father, who shook his hand and thanked him for visiting Jenny. Saskia pitied Joel, pitied the seriousness with which they were all forced to accord this visit, when they had yet to even, seriously, kiss. How was he not squirming under it all like a bug under a pin?

The doorbell rang. Saskia left Joel and her father to answer it. Marcel Bouchard stood at the door with a bouquet of iris for Jenny and a bottle of wine for the table. He had resumed his habit of dining with them weekly, and Saskia had purposely chosen his night to bring Joel around. Marcel Bouchard would be a buffer.

"How is she?" he asked, ritually, and Saskia answered, "The same."

"That's good." He hugged her briefly. "Now, where's this young man?"

Saskia had calculated correctly: Marcel Bouchard provided the warmth her father could not, and Joel relaxed visibly as the supper progressed. Her father's colleague spoke French with a broad Québécois twang,

Joel with anachronistic Acadian charm, and soon they were laughing and arguing loudly about the Habs. Saskia had made salad and pizzas with arugula and goat cheese and prosciutto. Pre-made crusts, pre-washed greens, a few fancy deli items, and it was all presentable enough. Good, even.

Her father didn't speak French. "You were cruel to bring him," he said quietly to Saskia, as the other two carried on. "You remind her of everything she can't have. Is this some kind of revenge?"

They had had this conversation already, when she had first proposed bringing Joel to meet Jenny, when she had first mentioned to her father that she was seeing some-one. Her father poured himself another glass of Marcel Bouchard's wine.

"I think she's happy for me," Saskia said. "She was always trying to get me to meet someone."

Her father reached over and caught her hand. "Selfish, just like your mother," he murmured. Joel, catching the gesture but not the words, smiled at Saskia.

At the end of the evening, Joel insisted she remain in the warm house with her family rather than drive him home. He would get a bus. It was no problem. On the doorstep, Saskia apologized for her father, but Joel shook his head. "You guys are so strong," he said, and kissed her hair as had become his habit. "Thank you for tonight. I'm so glad I got to meet her. Maybe I can come back again sometime?"

"You *are* a masochist." Saskia was ready for more than a kiss on the hair. "Maybe when my father's out, next time."

"No, I liked him. He's just—focused on Jenny. He doesn't have room right now for anything else. I get it. I'd like to get to know him better too."

"That's not what I meant," Saskia said.

The Christmas season came: strings of coloured lights in the rain, and the wise old owl's knitting went from baby pinks and blues to scarlet, evergreen, and gold. Saskia thought they might skip decorating the house this year since her mother was still away, but one afternoon her father surprised her by making the journey under the stairs himself to unearth the boxes of ornaments. They drove to the parking lot of a big-box hardware store to buy a tree for the corner of Jenny's room, and spent one twilight decorating it while she slept. The wise old owl produced scarves she had knitted each of them, one for Jenny, too, and chocolate oranges. Her father poured rum and eggnog and gave the wise old owl her gift, a generous bonus cheque. Saskia turned the television to the fireplace channel and they toasted the season. She thought the pale, celadon-green angora scarf made

Jenny's skin look wan, but her father's scarlet wool was handsome on him and he was a good sport to wear it as long as their party lasted. Her own dark green was all right.

She had pinned Jenny's childhood advent calendar to the wall by her bed and was pressing the windows open one by one with a fingertip, letting the forgotten images absorb her—the elf, the stocking, the apple—when the wise old owl set down her cup of eggnog and leaned forward to look at one of the monitors. Jenny opened her eyes.

"Hello, you," Saskia said.

Jenny died in hospital after all. After the seizure that ended their Christmas party, she closed her eyes and didn't open them again, though her body hung on for another month. The nurses, once kindly, now looked sidelong at the Gilberts when they came to visit. Eventually the family was asked to make a decision about life support.

"It should be Sassy's decision," her mother said, with the bleak clarity of new sobriety. "She's closer to Jenny than any of us. It will affect her the most."

Her father took a deep breath but said nothing. He, too, looked at Saskia.

Saskia was appalled. "Daddy, please."

But in the end it was indeed Saskia who spoke with the hospital lawyer, Saskia who spoke with Dr. Zhang, Saskia who sat with Jenny one last time. Afterwards it was Saskia who called the funeral home, Saskia who informed their extended family and friends, Saskia who arranged to pay the monstrous bill for the private room, Saskia who packed her sister's few effects into a plastic hospital bag and took them home. Saskia who booked the church and the restaurant and stipulated donations rather than flowers and dealt with the flowers that arrived anyway, Saskia who wrote the obituary, Saskia who delivered the eulogy. Saskia who held her father's arm and kissed her mother's cheek and accepted the mourners' condolences and suffered everyone to look on her face and see Jenny-not-Jenny, the person she was now, because—*shh*—it was actually Saskia who had gone down into the hole and would not come up again. Jenny was going to be just fine.

Professor Taillac was an asshole. "You know you could take a leave instead. Dropping out is a drastic decision when you are in a fragile state."

"I'm not fragile. I'm grieving."

"You are one of the most promising students I've had in a long time. That paper on the implications of consent in Réage was a breakthrough, no? Certainly I was hard on you at the beginning. Cécile said it would be good for you. I'm not quite such a monster as my reputation suggests. Already we've seen the dividends."

She could see he was pleased with that word, *dividends*. "My sister just died." Her voice was husky. "I'm not interested in pornography or erotica or whatever you want to call it. I'm not interested in anything right now."

Professor Taillac held her gaze for a long time and she suffered it to show she could. She understood he believed he was imparting something of immense, wordless importance. "I should like to loan you something," he said finally. "Something that was important to me at a difficult time in my life. When I was young, as you are now."

She watched him rise from his desk and go to the bookcase with the glass door. All the students in her program knew about that bookcase. He pulled a key ring from his pocket and opened the door with a small key, a tiny snick of metal going home. The books were arranged spine in. Professor Taillac seemed to know them all regardless, and selected a small, foxed volume with a faded green cardboard cover. He closed the bookcase, locked it, and returned to his desk.

"We take so much into us when we lose someone we

love," he said. "We must hold what is left of them. We make choices they would have made, feel what they would have felt. This is the piece of ourselves we lose, you see, because we must make room for them. Death is a parasite, of sorts." He set the book on the desk. "I bought this in Paris, before you were born, probably." He pushed it towards her, but waited until she reached for it, until both their fingertips were touching the cover, before releasing it. "You'll bring it back to me when you're ready, and then we'll resume your studies."

"My sister just died," Saskia repeated. Was the man a halfwit? Her old life was ended. Books—why? She expected it was some kind of filth.

"I care for you, Saskia." He tapped the cover with a fingertip. "We'll speak again."

They did not speak again; not for many years. Saskia didn't return to the University. Instead, she got a job at a café and found a basement apartment in the People's Republic of East Vancouver, just off the Drive. She took Jenny's clothes with her.

CHAPTER FIVE

Spring 2016

Sara didn't recognize him at first. He appeared in the doorway of her campus office, thin and obviously ailing, waiting for her to remember who he was. When his name caught up to her apprehension, she found herself inviting him to lunch. He'd be easier to get rid of once she knew what he wanted.

"Faculty club, Sara?"

"You need a reservation. I was thinking soup and sandwich in the Student Union Building. It's where I usually go."

"Soup and sandwich. I would certainly love a soup and sandwich."

He ate little, though, and seemed relieved when she tossed the last half of her tuna wrap so they could go outside, where he could smoke. Springtime: thin sun on wet pavement, the cherry blossoms just overblown.

"You don't look well," Sara said.

"That was probably the best soup I've ever tasted in my life. Some kind of vegan, vegetarian? Thai? These students have it good, eh?"

She said nothing.

"I found you on the University website. They list your office and phone number. Even a photo. So I knew it was the same Sara Landow. They make it easy for a stalker. What's it been, four years?"

"What can I do for you, Robert?"

"I'm not a stalker." He lit another cigarette. "I shouldn't have said that. I don't mean to scare you. I do need some help, but I'm not going to make this difficult."

"I don't think I can help you." Sara stopped walking. She wasn't going to take him back to her office. "You're supposed to stay away from us. Mattie and me."

"How is she?"

Sara said nothing.

"Don't you want to know where I've been all this time?"

Sara shook her head. "I know where you've been."

"All right, you checked. Of course you did." He nodded. "After I got out, though. After my parole ended. You know where I'm living?"

"No," Sara said softly.

"Well, the thing is, here and there." Robert nodded again and looked around the campus as though appraising it, hands on his hips. "Here and there. I was doing pretty good until a few months ago. Kindness of strangers and all that. But you're no stranger."

"I won't give you money. I have to teach a class. If you follow me, I'll call campus security."

"How is she?" he called after her. She didn't turn around. "How is she, Sara?"

The next time she saw him was in front of her building. He must have remembered her address from his time with Mattie; it had been on the corkboard next to the downstairs hall phone in her mother's house. She took out her cell and phoned 911.

"Ah, Sara." He backed away into the dusk. He didn't seem scared.

A police cruiser came by after a few minutes, by which time of course he was gone. She gave them his name and explained the history. She was told she'd done the right thing and to phone 911 again if he came back. They told her to keep detailed notes on every interaction and said she might want to consider getting an unlisted phone number. They asked if Robert Dwyer owned a gun. She didn't know. They drove away, and she went inside to make supper.

Mattie had already laid the table—one of her chores—and was watching a musical. She got up to hug Sara, then sat down again while Sara boiled pasta and heated a jar of tomato sauce in the microwave. The music made her grit her teeth.

"Could you please turn it down?" Sara said finally.

Mattie knew Sara's moods. She turned it far down, and sat tensely until Sara called her to the table. She got the shaker of Parmesan from the fridge without Sara asking and waited until Sara thanked her.

"How was work?" Mattie asked.

"All right. Donna says hello."

They ate spaghetti with tomato sauce and pre-washed salad from a bag. Sara lit the candles Mattie had set out and Mattie's eyes flared with pleasure. Sara's class that day had been on clinical counselling in genetics, ethics, and policy. She co-taught it with Donna August, the Associate Dean of Law, an austere woman who had turned down a judgeship to remain in academia. Donna wore a white brush cut and towering heels and severe little Mao-collared jackets she sewed herself. When Sara had mentioned the Robert situation to her, Donna remembered him. Sara had sought Donna's advice at the time so the annulment would be watertight.

"Oh Christ." Donna had stopped stacking papers and together they watched the last of the students file out of the lecture hall. "Poor Mattie."

Poor *Mattie?* Sara had thought.

"Do you remember Robert?" she asked Mattie now.

As she watched Mattie think, she wondered what five years looked like in her mind: what kind of taffy pull, what kind of synaptic flash. Yesterday confused her, but she remembered episodes from childhood with regrettable clarity.

"My Robert," she said finally.

"Have you seen him? Lately, I mean."

"He went away." Mattie frowned. "A long time ago."

"I know, sweetie."

"I miss him."

Mattie started to cry. Sara took her to the couch and hugged her miserably until she was ready to eat again. Sara opened the Malbec she had picked up on the way home, just to let it breathe. She had a rule about not starting until Mattie was in bed.

Over the next three months Robert appeared sporadically, but only when she was by herself. He asked for her money. He asked for her time. He asked her not to ignore him, not to disrespect him. He asked after Mattie. The fourth time the cruiser came too late, she asked the officers why they couldn't make it stop.

"We can't find him." But they were looking, they said. It was an active file. They had some leads. They asked if he'd said what he wanted the money for.

"Shelter. Medicine."

"Probably meth. You think meth?"

The thinness, the twitchiness, the sores on his face. "Probably meth," Sara said, though of course she wasn't that kind of doctor.

Finally she decided to tell Mattie, to warn her. She brought home ginger broccoli, glass noodles, and green tea ice cream.

"Listen, sweetie," Sara said.

Mattie seemed to understand, and not to mind, that Sara would accompany her to as many of her activities as possible from now on. She would walk her to workshop, and craft night, and her Community Living dances. Sara had negotiated a partial work-from-home arrangement with her dean until the matter was resolved. She could take her laptop to the dances and so on.

"Will he go to prison?" Mattie asked.

"I don't know." Sara started clearing the table. "I hope not. We've still got a restraining order—that means a judge will tell him to leave us alone. If he's good about that, he won't have to."

"I don't want him to." Mattie watched Sara take the ice cream from the freezer.

"I don't either." Sara dished them both bowls, her own portion smaller than Mattie's. She very badly wanted him to go away for a long time. One of these days the cruiser would make it in time. His harangues had been getting longer, lately, and she had started going outside with her phone in her hand, ready to speed-dial as soon as she saw him. One day he wouldn't notice, and would still be talking when the police came, and they would take him away.

After Mattie went to bed that night, Sara opened the wine and over the next couple of hours watched back-to-back episodes of a thriller she liked. A bleak farm in Sweden in November, an alcoholic detective, and a deranged killer sheltered by the sad old father who blamed himself. An ornate B plot gave the detective a troubled erotic life (he had particular tastes that had perhaps been informed by a woman who had perhaps died a long time ago). Each stark little episode featured brutal sex and lovely shots of the landscape in winter light. It was easy enough not to go to bed.

Half past late, Mattie drifted into the flickering blue light of the living room. Sara was finishing the noodles, saltier and tastier somehow for being cold from the fridge, and she still had a good fat glass left in the bottle. She led Mattie back to bed and returned to the TV to lower the volume.

The phone rang. "Look out your window," he said.

She kept the bedroom blinds closed but never those in the living room. She had a view of English Bay only partially blocked by the low-rise across the road. She could see her neighbours through their windows, and they could see her: eating, watching TV, working, reading.

What was there to hide? The windows were open to the mild blue late-June night. She looked out but couldn't see him. They were on the third floor. She heard footsteps that echoed strangely between her phone and the night she leaned into. He was close.

"I can't see you," she said.

He laughed and the footsteps stopped. "You're drunk."

The TV was paused on a scene of a frozen mud field stubbled with the husks of some blond crop. In the distance was a grey stone farmhouse. For a moment she couldn't remember what was happening in there, whether it was sad old father making tea on the hob or the killer dismembering a young girl or the detective taking it hard the way he liked. This episode, or the previous one, had featured each of these scenes.

"Good show?"

"I like it." She thought about throwing some money out the window, coins on the pavement, just to make him show himself.

"Mattie still sleepwalks."

"Are you asking me?"

She heard him swallow. "Come out and play."

"What are you drinking?"

"You wouldn't like it."

"Maybe I would."

Far away, a siren twirled up into the night.

"Fuck, Sara." He hung up.

She poured the fat glass and turned her show back on. It was the old father making tea. Green tea; the kind of detail that made it her show. The old Swedish farmer, dying of knowledge, drinking sencha for his health.

Sara and Donna August went perfume shopping. Donna had worn Cuir de Russie to their first class together last fall, and Sara had recognized it, and that had led to a conversation wherein they each confessed to this particularly intimate hobby. Donna August's preferences were earthy and assertive: tobacco, mushrooms, leather, civet. She savoured the shot silk effect of jasmine and shit. Umami, she would have called it, probably. Sara preferred the elusive, the fragile—watercolour flowers, tea, the wistfulness of pear. They shopped together a few times a year, and gave each other lists when one or other of them was going to Seattle and could get to Barneys or Rose de Mai. They traded samples and shared orders from Paris occasionally, also, but this was expensive, and Sara frankly did not like Donna knowing how much she was willing to spend. "An invisible dress," a Frenchman had called perfume. Maybe secrecy and shame were inevitable corollaries of such tastes.

"This." Donna waved a test strip of Shalimar at Sara:

orange, vanilla, smoke. They were looking for a birthday present for Mattie, Sara's justification for an afternoon alone with her friend. She had left Mattie at the
apartment with a movie and strict instructions not to
answer the phone or the buzzer. She was rather hoping
Robert would appear while she was with her friend so
she'd have a witness, though so far that had not been his
way.

"You don't think it's cloying?"

"Oh, it's so hot right now." Donna shrugged. "Who can
tell? She'll like the bottle, anyway." The iconic, gaudy,
tasselled blue-and-gold fan. Art deco, Sara reminded
herself, unchanged since its initial design in 1925. Still.

"I was thinking rose, maybe." They drifted, cultured,
sure of themselves. Sara could be this person with
Donna.

"How is she? With everything that's been going on."

"She's excited about her birthday. I've promised her a
cake from Fratelli's."

"Will she have friends over?"

"For tea, yes." Mattie had invited three ladies and
their staff from the community centre for the afternoon.
They would eat cake and watch one of Mattie's movies. She and Mattie had already been shopping for party
favours—sticker books, movie cards, funny socks.

In the end, Sara bought her sister a pretty pink bottle of Kelly Calèche: jasmine, mimosa, sweet pink rose,

leather. Donna insisted on buying the suffocating Shalimar. "Even for her just to look at on her dresser. Give her a big hug from Donna. Bring her to campus sometime and we'll have lunch, the three of us. Do you suppose she remembers me?"

"Oh, yes." They watched the sales assistant solemnly wrap the gifts. "She remembers things from years ago better than what she had for breakfast this morning. She'll be thrilled that you thought of her."

They went to a hotel for drinks so they could sit in nice armchairs and be served. It was their ritual. Everything so exquisite, so expensive, so hushed and plush and tasteful.

"You must be anxious, though," Donna said. "I'm anxious for you. Are you carrying pepper spray? Are you sleeping?"

"Better than you'd think." Sara pictured the bottle of Shalimar, imagined spritzing it in Robert's eyes. She saw him reeling backwards as she strode away in her little black dress, catwalk-style. "I honestly don't think he intends to hurt Mattie. Or me, for that matter. He never hurt her before, when he had the opportunity. That's got to count for something."

"People change. Was he an addict back then?"

"He told me he was clean. I think it might have been one of the nicer times in his life, actually, before I wrecked it for him."

Donna gave her the stony, patient-impatient look Sara had seen her give some of her duller students.

"He could have hurt me a hundred times over by now," Sara objected. "He knows where my office is. He knows where I live. In the last four months he's caught me alone more times than I can count, but he's never done anything but talk and run away. Eventually the police will catch up to him, and it'll stop. It's just a nuisance. I'm being extra-cautious for Mattie's sake, that's all. Eventually he'll give up on me and find someone else to harass."

Donna raised her glass and they drank to that.

"Mattie."

Her sister came out of the bathroom in her fuzzy robe and fuzzy slippers, drying her hair with a towel. She was anxious and listening with her big eyes. She held a towel to her head but stopped rubbing it. She couldn't rub and listen at the same time.

"The police just called. They found Robert. They're . . . going to talk to him for a bit. I can go to work today, and you can go to your drop-in like you always do. Isn't that good?"

The police had mentioned charging Robert with stalking and probably drug possession. He would be in a lockup somewhere, and the sisters could finally go on with their lives. After a quiet morning on her office couch with her iPad, Sara had lunch with a molecular biologist and a bioethicist at the one white-tablecloth restaurant on campus. They ate hundred-mile salads and her colleagues each had a glass of white wine. Sara had Pellegrino. They laughed a lot, and lingered over coffee. "August is my favourite," the bioethicist said. "No students, no marking, no rush. A little course prep, a little coffee, a little online shopping, am I right?"

Sara worked in her office into the gold-spackled light of the supper hour. She had a view of a quad landscaped with indigenous plants and artificially weathered benches and a winding path of concrete slabs, a legacy gift of some retired dean. There was a plaque that explained the significance of it all. Sara liked to see the few summer students sprawled over their books and listen to the pony-clop of footsteps echoing off the concrete as the shadows lengthened.

She stopped on the way home for Lebanese takeout: hummus, pita, bitter olives, chicken tawook, mujadara. Mattie liked chicken.

From a distance she could see old Mrs. Rutherford sitting on the steps of their building. She lived at the opposite end of the hall from Sara and Mattie, and had lived in that building longer than anyone else, since before her husband died fifteen years before. She attempted authority over the communal aspects of the building residents' lives—managing the potted geraniums and slipping prickly little notes under people's doors about recycling and loud music—but she was always kind to Mattie.

"Lovely evening," Sara called.

Closer, she saw Mrs. Rutherford's face.

"What happened?" Sara asked.

The funeral was neither as small nor as private as Sara had hoped. A vain hope, with all the news coverage, but her dismay grew as each new person stepped into the nave of the Anglican church their late mother had favoured. Friends of their mother's, friends of Mattie's, staff from the group homes where her friends lived, her own colleagues from the University, the police and para-medics who had first responded to the call, neighbours from their building, and utter strangers who had seen the news and thought their own condolences important. Sara delivered the eulogy, mentioning Mattie's love of musicals and praising her sweetness. When she looked up from her notes, the mourners offered brave smiles and nods of encouragement. She ended with the thought that they should remember Mattie as she had been in life, not in death, and that the world was a better place for having such souls in it. She felt a ripple, then, as the mourners looked without looking at the other Matties sitting amongst them.

A hand on her elbow on the steps of the church, just as she thought it was over: David Park.

They hugged. High school sweethearts, they had been—introverted, studious, ambitious. They had barely touched each other. Something had kindled briefly when she returned home at Christmas from her abortive first try at university in Toronto, but they had fought over her treatment of Mattie and he had ended it. They hadn't seen each other now in—how long had it been?

"I'm so sorry," he said into her hair, as though it were his fault. He was crying. He looked (Sara couldn't help noticing) lovely: that dark suit, those cheekbones.

"You smell nice," she said.

They went for a walk. Summer was crisping and browning, readying for fall despite the lingering heat.

She learned that he had become a surgeon (the plan since he was fourteen), and that his parents were both still alive. He was married. He still played the violin, and seemed perplexed and disappointed when she said she no longer kept up her piano. She told him about her career at the University, her mother's death, and the birthday Mattie had been looking forward to so much: the cake, the friends.

"I was unkind to you," David said. "You took care of

her right to the end. I'm the one who walked away. I underestimated you."

"Not quite to the end."

David stopped walking and so did she. He put his hands on her shoulders and turned her to face him. "None of this is your fault."

"I haven't cried. I can't cry."

"Shock."

She shrugged. "I just assumed they'd lock him up right away. I thought we were safe. It never occurred to me they'd question him and let him go."

He offered to drive her home in his immaculate Prius. A foil-wrapped casserole sat on her doormat, with a note from the gay couple two floors down. She put the casserole in the fridge.

"Show me her room," David said.

The bed, closet, dresser, stuffed animals, movie posters; the silly pretty chandelier, soft curtains, beads and baubles in a china dish, shoes, slippers, and the blue beaded wallet; the cup on the nightstand from her warm milk and cinnamon, one week ago now, the night before the last day.

"I'll help you with it," David Park said. "When you're ready."

In Sara's bedroom they finished what they had started a long time before. He was sure of himself in a way he'd never been when she'd known him. Married, she reminded herself. That must be where he'd learned it.

"You can help me with one thing today," she said as he tied his shoes.

"Anything."

"Take these." From the desk drawer she fetched the two gift-wrapped bottles of perfume. "Just—take them."

They hugged once more at the door. "Will you move? I mean, you're okay here by yourself? You wouldn't rather be in a hotel?"

"No."

It had been twenty-six years—she worked it out after he'd gone.

There had been many witnesses to the events of that August afternoon. One of Sara's neighbours, a young woman returning from work, saw Robert standing by the intercom. She had been afraid he would try to let himself in behind her, but he did not.

Another woman, parked across the street with her son in the back seat, saw Robert and Mattie talking on the sidewalk. She did not see where Mattie had come from. But the gay couple, headed for after-work drinks with colleagues on Denman Street, passed Mattie walking home. She smiled when they greeted her and seemed her normal, happy self. It was concluded from the keys found still zipped in her purse that she had stopped to speak with Robert in front of the building. She never made it inside.

Everyone who was home had windows open—it was a prewar building without central air conditioning—and once the shouting started several witnesses had gone to their windows to see what was going on. *You love me,* they remembered hearing, and *Don't you love me?* They saw Robert take Mattie by the shoulders, saw Mattie push him away. They saw Robert reach for her again, saw her jerk away from his touch and trip and fall backwards and hit her head on the concrete step and not get up.

Help, Robert had called. *Someone call 911.*

He had stayed while the neighbours ran outside to find him cradling her head in his lap, stayed while the ambulance came, stayed weeping until the police came and took him away. All this had happened just twenty minutes before Sara got home to find Mrs. Rutherford waiting for her on the steps. Sara had accidentally left her cell phone plugged into her charger at work, which was why no one had been able to reach her.

Mattie died in the ambulance of a cerebral hemorrhage right around the time Sara would have been stopping for Lebanese.

———

The coroner declared Mattie's death an accident. Robert pled guilty to criminal harassment. Sara saw him at sentencing. If he'd looked ill before, now he looked devastated. He wept frequently, and when he saw Sara he mouthed, "I'm sorry."

Sara did not give a victim impact statement.

In the end, the judge sentenced Robert to a year in jail. He took into consideration the fact that Robert had not fled the scene, he had called for help, he had waited for first responders, and his story was entirely corroborated by the many witnesses. Robert read a statement in which he confirmed he was attending Narcotics Anonymous and would remember Mattie's goodness every day for the rest of his life. He would give his own life to bring her back if he could. Anything Sara asked of him, he would do.

The movie played again and again in Sara's mind. "The police just called. They found Robert. They're . . . going to talk to him for a bit. I can go to work today, and you can go to your drop-in like you always do. Isn't that good?"

Mattie had stared at Sara, trying to understand.

"I'm going to work now," Sara said again, slower. "You'll be all right." It wasn't a question.

Mattie started to cry.

"No. Stop it."

Mattie went back into the bathroom, still crying, and closed the door.

Sara went to work.

At this point—trying to sleep, trying to eat, trying to concentrate on anything at all—Sara's mind always walked away from her own body, which was walking to the bus that would take her to campus, walked back into the apartment, and lived Mattie's last hours with her.

In the bathroom Mattie stood on the bathmat as she had been taught, because she was still dripping, and wept. She wept for her husband, and for her sister who was so mean, who made her so lonely. She looked in the mirror and saw her face all ugly with crying, and that made her cry harder. She turned away so as not to see herself and there was the empty rail. She hung her towel as she had been taught, and then she squeezed a dab of styling creme into her palm to tame the frizzies, as Sara had taught her. Mattie had the frizzies because she was curly. The creme smelled like coconut.

She hung the bathmat over the lip of the tub as Sara liked it and went to her room to dress. Clean under-wear. Smell your bra, if it's smelly put it in the hamper and Sara will wash it by hand when she has time. Wear a nude bra under a light-coloured blouse, then it won't show. Wear a slip, then your underwear won't show. Ladies wear skirts. Her mother had taught her that.

Mattie had to cry again a little to think of her mother, who had loved her all her life and sang to her in her frail quavering voice, and didn't mind when Mattie sang along. Mattie wore her blue skirt and a white blouse and leather shoes, not sneakers, because ladies didn't wear sneakers. Mattie couldn't remember whether that was her mother or Sara. She wore the soft white cardigan with the white blouse.

In the hallway, as she was locking the door with her key, she heard someone grumbling around the corner. It was old Mrs. Rutherford, whose son had married an Oriental. She always had a smile for Mattie, though, and told her she looked very fresh and pretty today.

They waited together for the elevator.

"Someone is erasing names from the sign-up sheet in the laundry room again," Mrs. Rutherford said.

"Uh-oh," Mattie said.

Mrs. Rutherford had some more to say about that while the lights above the door walked to the left, past all the numbers. Now they were on the ground.

"You'll tell your sister," Mrs. Rutherford said.

"Sara." Mattie didn't know what Mrs. Rutherford wanted her to tell Sara, but Sara would know.

Mrs. Rutherford thanked her, and began the slow business of finding her mailbox key in her pocket. Mattie said goodbye and walked outside.

At the bus stop she lined up behind five people. She

was number six. Number five was an Oriental staring at his phone. Mattie smiled at him but he didn't see. When the bus came, Mattie showed her pass and the driver nodded. She smiled at him.

The only free seats were the ones at the front, for the elderly and disabled. Mattie went to the back and stood with her legs far apart for balance, the way Sara had taught her. Sara had bought her a bag that hung diagonally across her body by a good strap so she would have both hands free to hold on. Their mother had not thought of that, but their mother had never ridden the bus. Sara had wanted her to choose the black one but Mattie had wanted the yellow. Inside the yellow cross-body bag was her blue beaded wallet and some tissues and the phone that was not for using like the Oriental used his, only for emergencies. It was a less complicated phone. Mattie pulled it out to look at sometimes, even though Sara had told her not to, because there might be a message. Mattie didn't know what a message would look like, but one day there might be a word on the screen, that would be it: Message. One day.

Drop-in was busy, and today was lunch program. Her friends were happy to see her. Karen, one of the staff, wondered where Sara was and Mattie told her Sara had gone to work. Karen looked at Toby but Toby said Sara had already called him and he would explain later and it was fine.

Mattie sat with her friends and made a bird feeder. When Karen and David called them for lunch, they went and had sandwiches and juice and her friends who had medications took their medications. After lunch was yoga stretches and then bingo.

"You're thoughtful today," Karen said to her while she waited for them to call the numbers. Karen was sitting at her table.

"I'm all right," Mattie said.

Karen put her arm around Mattie's shoulders and gave her a squeeze, a hug with one arm.

"Someone is erasing the names from the sign-up sheet in the laundry room again," Mattie told her.

"That's no good," Karen said.

At four o'clock it was time to go home. Mattie had won a sticker book at bingo. The stickers were shiny foil Easter eggs and bunnies even though it was August because it was almost her birthday. She put it in her cross-body purse for later. Her purse had a zip, that was safe.

The bus home was very busy and it was hard to stand wide. When she stumbled, a man stood up and offered her his seat. She smiled at him. He was an Oriental. Sara had told her not to say "Oriental" because it was rude. She said it was their mother's word and their mother had been old-fashioned about some things and people from Asia were not from another planet for god's sake. *What about David Park?* Sara said, and Mattie remembered David Park. He was an Oriental too. He had been their friend.

The walk from the bus stop to home was hot and by the time Mattie got to the steps of their building she thought she might have a big glass of cold water once she got upstairs. That would be all right: a big glass of cold water.

But on the sidewalk in front of her building stood her Robert.

He was already talking and kept talking as he walked towards her, making her stumble back in surprise. He was talking very fast and she couldn't understand and she wanted a hug but he was talking so fast, and finally she understood he wanted money. He was yelling, why was he yelling? He was pointing his finger at Mattie, jabbing his finger, talking so fast. He got up close to her but not to hug or kiss. He was yelling. She stepped back.

"You love me, don't you love me?" he was yelling.

Mattie put her hands over her ears. She felt some spit from his mouth land on her cheek and she started to cry.

PART TWO

CHAPTER SIX

August 2017

High above the cathedral doors, Sara sees or thinks she
sees (she is drunk), a gargoyle: hands working between
withered frog-legs, wings spread, head thrown back. She
imagines some red velvet hell, some masturbatorium
where he suffers with his kind. She is in Paris, finally,
again, and Mattie has been dead for a year. Sweet Mattie
is with the worms, and Sara would like a drink please.
Europeans drink; it's elegant. It's not a problem.

The joke being that she has been to Paris only once
before, with her mother and sister; drunk Stella Artois
in the Galeries Lafayette, the drinks counter overlook-
ing the perfume floor, while her mother bought Mattie
clothes, and everyone so nice. She had been drinking
even then, she realizes, ten years ago. Agnès b., her

mother's taste: wool, cashmere. Navy, charcoal, black. Everyone so kind. And why not? What did it cost anyone to be kind? Mattie was hardly a unicorn. Retarded girls wore clothes in Paris too. She had got her mother drunk on that trip, and Mattie tipsy. She was going to hell. This was on their last night, at a restaurant around the corner from their rental flat. You are not driving, their waiter kept saying. No, we're not driving. The fish was exquisite, the beef bloody, heavenly. Her tongue came. Mattie giggled. Maybe her tongue came too.

An alcoholic, Sara. Everyone knew, no one knew. A red-wine drunk, Sara, and the occasional cognac. That was all. The French, she would say to Mattie, trying to explain, and Mattie would smile expectantly. Certainly, the French. Sara was a drunk.

In her mind she lives alone, somewhere old and elegantly seedy: Lisbon, Venice, or some old Caribbean port where the sun dawns pinkly and the trade winds cool the veranda in the evening. White threadbare curtains fluttering. Or grey stone in winter, cold damp rooms with wallpapers rococo with mold, and in a single room a fire in a fireplace, a blanket on a sofa, a glass of red wine. In her mind she remains an alcoholic, but refined and functional and private. She isn't sloppy. She wears beautiful clothes and jewels and scent, diamonds and furs, and somehow is not ridiculous. In the Caribbean version she drinks at dusk and writes on a vintage pink typewriter before that, beautiful stern short stories that sell in important places none of the locals read. She has wealth, privacy, solitude, and such lovely, lovely clothes.

The waiter at Le Hibou brought Sara her wine and two black ramekins, one of salted peanuts and the other of green clingstone olives. Lunch! She ordered a carafe of water, too, like the *sophistiquée* she was. No book this time, but sunglasses, leaning back in the cane chair, tapping a short, blood-red fingernail on the zinc pizza of a table, watching the passersby. She'd had her nails done by an Algerian girl in a cupboard in the Marais on a Sunday, that was yesterday or the day before, not far from the Place des Vosges. Only the Marais was open on Sunday. Blood red was too dark for August. She'd have them redone in another day or so, when they started to chip. Pearl grey, maybe. Blood and brains, yes. She was aware. It was too hot for red wine, also, but August in Paris—who was there to judge? Who was there to judge her drinking and shopping and beautifying on the first anniversary of her sister's death?

———

David Park, for one. He had not wanted her to go.

"That's all you're taking?" He had offered to drive her to the airport, and had come early to watch her pack.

"I'll shop there."

He shook his head so she didn't tell him of her plan, which pleased and excited her inordinately: to take only the clothes on her back, and buy a new outfit each day to wear the next. Toiletries too. She was going with nothing. An empty suitcase to bring it all back in.

He guessed anyway. "But you already have so many clothes."

"You already have so many CDs." Their old argument.

Anyway, she did not have so many clothes. She *curated* and *edited* her *collection* relentlessly. Terms she found on websites devoted to fashion; literary terms, oddly appropriated. Oddly appropriate, she corrected herself. She spent a lot of money on very little: a jacket here, a bracelet there. Four or five *pieces* a year. Like an elderly librarian in a tall stone tower, adding incremental preciousness to her collection of rarities. This splurge would be an anomaly.

"Hey, come here." David Park was sitting on her bed while she stood in her underwear, deciding what to wear on the plane. And after a while, "Don't go."

"I'm not going to spend my vacation sitting around

Vancouver waiting for you to sneak away from Alice."
Their other, more recent argument.

"No. You're going to commemorate Mattie's death
with shopping."

"Shopping *and* drinking," before he could say it. They
had a lot of arguments, actually. "You know, I can take a
cab to the airport."

"That would probably be better." David Park looked
at his watch.

The night man at the hotel desk greets her every evening in French. He knows she is Canadian and an anglo-
phone, but she's been trying since the day she arrived,
and he honours her effort. He is respectful. On her first
night she had to bring her bottle down because there was
no corkscrew in the room. He opened it expertly, running the tip up the foil to score it, popping the cork with
that lovely, holy, popping sound, then handing her back
both bottle and corkscrew. Keep it! But no, Madame,
there should have been one in the room, of course there
should. It was the hotel's mistake entirely. No, he would
not take a glass for thanks, but it was genial of her to
offer. Good night, Madame.

Long night, Madame. Her room overlooks the Carre-
four de l'Odéon, a busy little triangular intersection of
cafés, bars, restaurants, shops, hotels. There is Le Hibou,
just there. Her hotel features a famous restaurant on the
ground floor. Her window is veiled by pink flowers that
grow in the window boxes outside, such that she can sit
on the floor and look out and drink only a few feet above
the heads of passersby without being seen, when she has
passed the stage of sitting presentably at Le Hibou and
needs to go on alone.

She walks each day until her feet speak to her. *Why?* her
feet ask. *Oh, please, why?* Then she sits in a café. She always
has a book so no one will talk to her, though it seems
there is little danger of that in any case. She goes to gal-
leries, museums. She stares at the Art. She thinks about
what Mattie would have liked, what Mattie would have
understood. That painting with the horse: she would
have liked the horse, but because it was a horse, not
because it was a painting. She would have been bored by
the rooms of broken pots. Sara decides she, too, is bored
by the rooms of broken pots. But is her boredom more
genuine than Mattie's? That is a question.

In her sober moments—early in the morning, reading in a café with sunglasses and ibuprofen, unsweet milky coffee, the washed streets, the horizontal dawning light, the recycling trucks, the storefront grates rolling up, the sharp early-morning ring of footsteps and everything, the pink and blue of everything—she reads *Au château d'Argol* by Julien Gracq. Young people drunk on Hegel, sleeping on furs, arguing philosophy, in a bizarre castle perched above a great and sinister forest. It tests her French punishingly, and in these early mornings is a source of profound pleasure. She sleeps poorly. The coffee is a help. The waiters let her be. "It *is* a pretty colour," she says one morning, aloud, to Mattie; her sister commenting on the blood-red cover of her book because she can share no other part of it. The waiters look at her. After that she cannot go back to the Café de Flore.

In the Jardin de Luxembourg she sits for a long time at the mouth of the cool green tunnel that is the Medici fountain, thinking about David Park. Thinking, luxuriously, after sex with David Park, as he lay sleeping and she lay awake: I have made a mistake. She remembers blowing him to sleep and then drinking and watching TV. Plunging into the colours of red wine: cherries and smoke, chocolate, pepper. She tried to tell him about the spider in *Dr. No,* velvety and big as a rodent. The spider in *Through a Glass Darkly.* Was he sleeping? Oops. Was he sleeping?

Grey and cognac. Those are Sara's colours. She goes shopping at the *grands magasins* on the Boulevard Hauss-mann. In the Galeries Lafayette she attempts a form-fitting grey dress from a house with a name so famous it might as well have been the House of Atreus. The assistant's glance passes coolly over Sara's tummy. *"Mais non,"* Sara says impatiently, dismissing the dress, as though the fault is the assistant's, the designer's, and the assistant hastens to agree. A bit of theatre, all good fun. This shirt dress, now, though, somewhere between charcoal and chocolate, the very colour of sleep. *"Alors, Madame,"* the assistant says. *(This is much better for you, at your age.)* The shoulders fit precisely, the collar features her col-larbones, the sleeves end early to show off a pretty bracelet, the skirt flares from a trim leather belt. She could wear it for her shopping tomorrow, and at home it would do into the fall with a cardigan. She could undo the buttons for David Park, and do them back up when he was done. Their sex has been increasingly violent lately as they try and fail to let each other go.

———

At the hotel, the night man greets her with a smile that fades when he looks more closely at her face.

"I will tell you," Sara says in French. "It is the anniversary of my sister's death. I came here to get away. I have had too much to drink." A card she can only play once, but no matter. "I started to cry in Le Hibou. It was very embarrassing."

The night man looks stricken. He offers his condolences in French and then again in English, to make sure she understands.

"It's been a year. You would think—"

The night man shakes his head. "A year is nothing."

"It was my fault." Sara steps away from the desk as an elderly couple come in from the street and request their heavy brass room key with its maroon tassel. They glance at Sara, glance away, and go to the elevator. "I was supposed to take care of her."

"Absolutely not." The night man comes around the desk and offers his arm. "I will take you up to your room. With your permission, I will bring you a piece of bread and a cup of warm milk and cinnamon, and then you will sleep. Tomorrow will be better."

At Le Hibou, the waiter from yesterday greets her with a smile and asks if she would like the same. Thank you, yes. She has of course only imagined the scene with the night man: her tears, her penitence, his offer of a piece of bread and a cup of warm milk and cinnamon. It was what her mother would make for her when she was little and sad. She puts the bag with the dress on the chair next to her and throws her scarf over it to obscure the logo of the House of Atreus so it won't look like she's showing off.

When she was little and sad. So often; so often. Her mother seemed proud of Sara's precocious sadness, and told her repeatedly about Churchill's black dogs. Sara's father had left many biographies of Churchill on the shelf in his office. Sadness was a sign of great creativity and intelligence, that was the gist. Mattie, for instance, was rarely sad.

A mother sits down at the next table with a teenage girl and a toddler boy. Sara obligingly removes her shopping from the chair so the little boy can have it. The teen notices the logo and her eyes flicker over Sara. The little boy bursts into tears. He does not want to sit with the strange woman. He wants to sit on his mother's lap.

"Mais non." The mother's pretty, dark-haired and dark-eyed, in a silk summer dress and heels. The teen wears heels also, jeans, and a blazer. *"Assieds-toi, Olivier,"* the teen says. The little boy holds his arms up to her instead, so she pulls him onto her lap. *"Petit menace."* She kisses his dark hair. The mother pulls a magazine from

her bag and lays it on the table so they can all see it. She turns the pages and occasionally points at an image, or the teen does. The little boy's Orangina arrives with a tiny red straw. The teen and the mother get espressos. The teen slides the boy onto the chair she was sitting in and raises her eyebrows at Sara. Sara gestures towards the empty chair, *please*. The girl pulls it a little closer to their own table, takes out a phone, and begins to text. The little boy slides his eyes over to Sara and inches closer to his mother when he sees her looking.

Mattie had wanted a phone so badly. Sara liked the idea of an iPhone because the built-in GPS would always show where Mattie was. But Mattie lost that phone, and the next one. Either the missing phones were destroyed or whoever found them disabled the GPS because Sara was never able to locate them. After that Sara bought her cheap flip-phones, and Mattie lost those too. A dozen phones, maybe, in the five years they lived together. Sara would get bitterly angry about these losses, though the cost was negligible.

The little boy, Olivier, has grown bored with his mother's magazine and tugs on his sister's sleeve until she yields the phone and sets up a game for him with the sound turned off. Brightly-coloured cartoon figures drift across the screen while the boy, moving his entire upper body, attempts to arrest them somehow, tagging or shooting. The teen returns to looking at the magazine with the mother, their heads almost touching, murmuring.

Sara and her mother were never close like that. Of course there were reasons, reasons Sara had been able to appreciate since she was younger than this teen is now. Sara's father died when Sara and Mattie were still children, and that was hard. Seeing to Mattie had been a full-time job for their mother. She had taught Mattie to read when the school had given up. She had nursed Mattie through the bronchial infections that plagued her every winter, and guarded her virtue relentlessly as soon as it became apparent how pleasing she would grow to be. How eager to please. Twelve, thirteen? Mattie was the pretty one but Sara was the smart one, which meant her virtue was her own business. If she did not make trouble for her mother, her mother would not make trouble for her, that was the understanding. Her mother had required of Sara straight A's and a career plan. She didn't have space in her head or her heart for more.

The little family left without Sara noticing. Now their table is taken by two businessmen talking politics and smoking into their beer.

So you resent your mother? she imagines being asked, while she lies on a worn red velvet couch with the back of one hand pressed to her forehead. *What about the piece of bread and the cup of warm milk and cinnamon?*

Sara responds in her thoughts. Of course my mother cared for me. Of course she loved me. Of course we had some moments. I'm just saying we weren't close. Especially as I got older.

What about Mattie? the voice asks.

What about her?

Were you close?

You can't be close with someone like that.

No?

Well, what does it mean to be close? Sharing things that matter? I couldn't share anything with Mattie that mattered to me. Books, art, fashion, and my work, later.

Those are the things that mattered to you?

What else?

Dreams, maybe? Feelings? Hopes?

Now the businessmen are gone and it's two younger men, a couple. Scarved, sandalled, dapper in their cool linen shirts and rolled-cuff pants. They, too, smoke, over a bottle of blanquette de Limoux. The waiter stands the ice bucket next to their table.

Love? Sara thinks, mocking, vicious. My feelings for David Park?

Why not?

Because Mattie loved him too?

No, the voice says. The first thing the voice says that's not a question. *She wanted to marry someone else. She did marry someone else.*

That wasn't marriage.

Wasn't it?

Sometimes the voice belongs to David Park, sometimes to her sharp, dry, clever friend Donna August. Really of course the voice is her own—her conscience, those neurochemicals. She's chained in the masturbatorium of her own guilt, clawing at her own pinkest places.

"It's my fault," Sara tells Donna August. "I killed her," she tells David Park. She's lying on the hotel bed with the TV on low, a soccer game. There's no more wine, the room spins, she'll sleep soon. The sun sets slowly. It might be seven or eight. She'll wake deep in the night with a throbbing head and a dry mouth and lie awake, going back there again and again.

"The police just called. They found Robert. They're . . . going to talk to him for a bit. I can go to work today, and you can go to your drop-in like you always do. Isn't that good?"

She imagines Robert in his Hastings Street room no bigger than a cupboard. He can touch the door from his bed. He leaves the room unlocked at all times because he owns nothing but the clothes on his back. He eats at the soup kitchen, vomits it up in the alley, and staggers back to his room, to bed. He's sick, he's feverish. He's got a throbbing head and a dry mouth. He's not well.

Increasingly he's afraid of other people. Or not afraid. They horrify him, or bore him. He behaves stupidly around them, picking fights, joking meanly, demanding to be left alone. He has no plan. On days of nervous energy he walks from the Downtown Eastside to the West End, by the park, where the sisters live.

"The police just called. They found Robert. They're . . . going to talk to him for a bit. I can go to work today, and you can go to your drop-in like you always do. Isn't that good?"

She scribbles through her memories, her imaginings, assorted rags and scraps, bloody fringe from the trial. Now she's the young neighbour slipping past Robert through the door of their building. Now she's the gay couple heading for that patio, smiling at Mattie as they pass, arriving ahead of their friends and ordering a bottle of blanquette de Limoux. The waiter stands an ice bucket on a pedestal beside their table. Now she's the woman parked across the street. She texts a friend before passing her phone to the little boy in the back seat. She starts the car and notices Robert and Mattie when she shoulder-checks to pull into the street.

"The police just called. They found Robert. They're . . . going to talk to him for a bit. I can go to work today, and you can go to your drop-in like you always do. Isn't that good?"

Now she's reaching for her sister. (The church bells ring out 2:45 a.m., 3:00 a.m., 3:15 a.m. The streets are quiet.) This is the place she always works her way back to, the scab she has to pick. She's reaching for her sister but Mattie is recoiling. Now she's shouting and Mattie is crying, not because she's scared but because someone is angry with her, someone is always angry with her, Sara is always angry with her, and nothing she can do ever makes things right. Now Mattie's falling backwards, now her dumb fucking head hits the concrete step with a snap, like the last piece of a puzzle finding home.

"You wanted her dead," imaginary David Park says. "He did you a favour. You wanted her out of your life."

"I wanted her at a distance," Sara admits.

"You should never have taken her in. There were alternatives, surely."

"Group homes. Care."

"Care," David echoes.

"My mother never wanted that for her. She was afraid of farming her out to strangers. That's what she called it."

"Strangers who might be nice to her."

"Stop it. Just stop."

"You shouted at her. You made her cry. You made her feel useless, like she was a burden. You didn't love her."

"That's supposed to be an accusation?"

"Someone else might have loved her. Might have cared for her and loved her enough."

"Robert?"

"You yourself admit he treated her well. Spoke kindly to her. Kept her clean and well fed. Could have had sex with her and didn't."

"He wanted the house. The money."

"Sure, probably." David shrugs.

"He didn't love her. He told me he didn't."

"Well, you had that in common, then."

"You keep coming back to that. You can love someone and be impatient with them. You can love someone and get frustrated. You can love someone and know it makes no difference."

"Tell me about it," David Park says.

The truth was that she *was* mean to Mattie, she *was* impatient, she was at times very, very cruel. *You've taken too much cereal again. You need to shower, you smell. Oh, give it to me, let me do it, I can't stand watching you. Please turn that off. Please stop talking.*

Her mother was never like this with Mattie, never, though she was condescending and judgmental and passive-aggressive and awful with everyone else. It was as though she'd had a single switch in herself that she'd flipped the moment she realized what Mattie was going to be. She'd flipped it to *patience*, she'd flipped it to *kindness*. She never raised her voice to Mattie, never held a grudge against her, never resisted a hug. Mattie got all she had, the little she had.

"Mattie made your mother better," David says. They have had this conversation, or conversations like it, many times. It didn't matter anymore if he was in her bed or in her head. "Without Mattie, what would she have been? A bitter, angry, self-pitying woman. What little nobility she had, Mattie forced it out of her."

"Can you praise someone for it, if it has to be forced out?"

"I'm not praising your mother, believe me." He had loathed their mother. "I'm saying if she was nice to Mattie, yes, that was a good thing."

"No matter the cost."

"What cost?" David Park hates her in moments like these, she knows. Sees nothing but her mother in her. Bitter, angry, self-pitying.

"The cost to—to her own identity. Who she could have been."

He's angry now. "Tell me, Sara. Who could *you* have been? Who could you have been without Mattie in your life? Tell me all you've suffered."

"Never mind."

"Tell me all the opportunities you've had to turn down. Tell me all the jobs that were refused you. Tell me about your life of poverty and disenfranchisement and abuse." He's breathing hard, on the razor's edge between shouting and tears. "You and your family are the most privileged, entitled people I've ever known. You have money and education and power, you travel, what you spend on clothes could put a kid through college. Selfishness, all selfishness."

"You're spluttering."

"How did she hurt you? Tell me one way."

Sara goes perfume shopping. She wears the dress the colour of sleep, the leather belt, heels. Sunglasses. No scarf, no jewellery. She needs her wrists, and maybe her throat if she finds something she likes.

In the Palais Royal she walks along the arcade. The

shop she's looking for is miniscule, with only one or two flacons on display and two assistants, an older woman and a younger, as well as a third woman in a smock, dusting, dusting. This is a shop where you have to ask for what you want, specifically, and if you don't know, you don't go there. You don't ring that bell, and they don't let you in.

Sandalwood: Sara wants sandalwood. *Santal.* There are three. The younger woman fetches them from the back and presents them to the older woman, who arranges them on a felt-topped table.

The first is sandalwood and bitter cacao. A bestseller, the older woman murmurs, almost apologetically. A *gourmand,* rich and refined, but very approachable. Very nice for the fall, for the first cold days. A *permanent* in the collection. It will never go out of style.

The second is sandalwood and rose. Sara hesitates over this one, for of course rose was Mattie's flower. Sweet and light and thin, very nice for spring. Dries down sweet and creamy. Here, one on one wrist, one on the other. You see the difference? Unavailable outside of France, the rose. A limited release from six months ago. Once the stock is sold off, it will disappear forever.

The third is sandalwood and cinnamon. A unisex, the woman says, not so sweet, and of course for this reason and because it is the third flacon—like something in a fairy tale—Sara decides it will be the best. She hands Sara a *touche* and the moment Sara smells it she starts to weep.

But Madame must not apologize. She would be surprised how many have this reaction, not to cinnamon necessarily, but each has her—you say in English—her trigger? Scent is a powerful trigger for memory, this is known. This is the perfumer's art. The younger woman nods. The woman in the smock nods. Sara accepts a tissue.

"Why *santal*?" the older woman asks kindly, earnestly. "Why *santal* today?"

At the hotel, the night man greets her with a smile that fades when he looks more closely at her face.

"I will tell you," Sara says in French. "It is the anniversary of my sister's death. I came here to get away. I have had too much to drink. I started to cry in a shop, a parfumerie. It was very embarrassing."

The night man looks wary. He offers his condolences in French and then again in English, to make sure she understands.

"She was murdered," Sara says. She touches the top button on her new dress and of course the man's eyes go there.

"Madame," he says. He comes from behind the counter and offers his arm. "I will take you to your room. You will sleep now, and in the morning you will feel better."

She tells him she prefers the stairs to the elevator. (An elderly couple got in the elevator.) On the landing, she puts her back to the wall and raises her skirt. He's startled and perhaps therefore not quick, and as he labours the sour, end-of-day smell of him gets stronger. She's too drunk for her own pleasure. Several layers of what feels like cotton batting insulate her from that, or indeed much sensation at all.

Early the next morning she chooses a place she hasn't been to yet, across the street from Le Hibou. Les Éditeurs, it's called: Café of the Editors. Inside are red leather club chairs, a giant's eye of a wall clock, books. She learns from a note on the menu that the place is favoured by people in publishing. A croissant, coffee, a glass of grapefruit juice, a glass of champagne. *"Un anniversaire,"* she tells the waiter, who bows. She has decided to buy a red dress today. She wears yesterday's purchases: the sandalwood, the white plissé skirt, the black cashmere sweater, the cinnamon silk scarf. Her hair is washed. She doesn't look too rough, though she was up long before dawn, waiting for the rest of the world to catch up. Here now is her champagne. She raises it to her lips, thinking of Mattie, still alive one year ago this morning.

David Park would have shaken his head at champagne for breakfast.

Lighting money on fire, he would have said, or something like that.

Oriental stinginess, her mother's voice says. *Like Jews, those immigrant families. Well, you can understand it, I suppose, coming from nothing. Did I tell you about the time—*

Yes, Sara says.

—the time I saw one trying to haggle the price of fish in Safeway? An Oriental, I mean. I don't think Jews shop at Safeway, it's not kosher.

No, Sara says.

Their mother had a teak dressing table with a centre panel that flipped up into a mirror, revealing the compartment where she kept her treasures. When they were little, Sara and Mattie would take these out one by one. Her wedding and engagement rings, too loose on her since the ravages of her young widowing—plain gold and gold set with a modest sapphire. They tried them on. "They'll be yours one day," their mother would say, watching them.

Mattie never heard the singularity of that "you," but Sara did. She felt the burden of it.

There was the garnet necklace. There were the pearl earrings in the grey box. Sara hated pearls. She shivered to touch them. Blind eyes. "Those will have to be yours, then, Mattie," their mother said. "I'll take them in someday and have them converted to clips so we won't have to get your ears pierced."

The Chanel No. 5, always kept in its box, and the 4711 for everyday. The gold-trimmed volume of *Funk & Wagnalls New Encyclopedia* in which their mother pressed flowers. A few leftover shillings and francs from her London-and-Paris honeymoon. A wooden bead bracelet on a red cotton string, bought impulsively from an African vendor on Granville Island and never worn. A set of white lawn handkerchiefs, still in their box, embroidered with a cardinal, a robin, a lark, and a thrush. A potpourri posy in a painted china thimble—a doll's bouquet, fragrant with cinnamon and cloves. Two fans: an ivory one from Hong Kong that their father had bought in Chinatown and a carved sandalwood one from Mysore, India, one of fifty their parents had given as keepsakes at their wedding. The ivory fan was kept wrapped in tissue paper, but the sandalwood—perforated with hundreds of tiny holes to make a pattern of flowers—came in a long green-gold box.

She had never hated her sister. If anyone had asked, she would have said she loved her. When they fanned each other, the ivory was always Mattie's, the sandalwood Sara's. Mattie would close her eyes and breathe the smell—that creamy wood smell—and open her eyes, and smile.

She phones David Park. He can hear it in her voice. "Come home."

"Hear what?"

"You're drunk."

"I've been phoning and phoning, but I always get Alice. I've been hanging up."

"Yes. We know."

There will be a problem when she gets home, and then there will be a solution. That's what she hears in *his* voice.

"I've bought some pretty dresses. Pretty frocks. With my pin money."

"Please, Sara."

"Please what?"

"You're going to kill yourself."

Sara laughs in astonishment and delight. "I could." There will be a problem, and then there will be a solution. A red velvet suicide.

"You were her better self," David says. "And she was yours."

Sara hangs up the phone. *I was her punishment, certainly,* she thinks, taking the empty suitcase out from under the bed. *As she was mine. But remind me again of our crime?*

CHAPTER SEVEN

November 2017

On a Monday night in November, Saskia came home to her basement apartment to find Marcel Bouchard leaning against the door. She had been swimming at the community centre, and was conscious of her damp hair. Her father's colleague hugged her, and she realized in that warm, wordless moment that she was standing on another black line separating before and after. Before and after what?

"It was quick," he told her, over tea he made in her kitchenette. She sat at the table watching the steam from her mug. "No pain."

"No pain." Saskia held the words in her mouth while she waited for her brain to catch up. "Who was driving?"

Her mother. But that was wrong. Her mother never drove.

"I haven't seen them in a year," Saskia said.

Marcel Bouchard took her hand. "I guessed, although we never talked about it, Hugh and I. He loved you very much."

"After I dropped out of school, after I moved out, he said I was throwing my life away. Each visit was worse than the last. Finally I stopped going. My mother called once or twice since the last time I saw them but I never called back. My father never called."

"Il t'aimait," her father's colleague repeated. He was from the suburbs of Montreal originally and always used to speak French with her, starting in Grade Six when she joined an immersion program. It had meant a bus ride alone to the public school rather than a walk with her mother and sister to the private school. It was a time when Jenny's erratic behaviour eclipsed Saskia entirely in her parents' minds. Jenny would skip school and refuse to tell anyone where she went all day. She would sneak out through her bedroom window at night. She was caught with cigarettes, fireworks, vodka, boys, girls. Marcel Bouchard saw all of this; he used to come regularly to the house for supper. He had just been through a divorce and was melancholy in those days. He was wary around Jenny, but his face lit up when he could speak French with Saskia.

He was talking now about legal matters, the funeral, the house, the will. He would help her with everything. He trailed off when he realized she wasn't taking it in.

"Why don't you come home with me tonight? Christine wanted me to ask you." He had remarried some years ago, a kindly woman who had just retired as a provincial court judge.

Saskia stared at him. She had heard the words, and was waiting for their meaning to sink in.

"Viens." Marcel Bouchard led her to the bathroom and found her toiletry bag under the sink. He told her what to put in it. He got her backpack from the closet and supervised her packing of a couple of days' worth of clothes. But when the cab came, she asked him to take her to her parents' house instead.

They had died abroad, on vacation in Scotland. Scotland in November—who but her father? A distillery tour, an unfamiliar rental car, the wrong side of the road. The family home was locked up tight, but fortunately the security code—hers and Jenny's birthdate—was unchanged and Saskia was able to disarm the house alarm before it occurred to her that her parents might have changed it without telling her. Marcel walked her inside while the cab idled at the curb. "Are you sure?" he said.

"I feel numb, that's all." The truth. "I'd like to—have them around me, tonight, I guess. Look at photo albums, stuff like that. I'll call you tomorrow, if that's okay. I understand there's going to be a lot to do."

"You're not alone in this world, Saskia." Marcel

hugged her. "Christine and I love you. We have a big place. You could move in with us if you wanted. Even just for a few months." He hesitated. "You know, it's okay to cry."

Once he was gone, she got the photo albums from the bottom of the bookcase in the front room and set them on the kitchen island. It didn't all have to be lies, not tonight. But leafing through them made her restless. She had turned these same pages not so long ago, it felt like, for Jenny, holding them so her sister could see and narrating their contents. There were no surprises left here, no feelings she wasn't ready for.

Her father's office had changed little since she last saw it, except that it was diminished. In her mind, the office was the brain of the house, throbbing and outsized. In reality it was a small room, overdecorated in a fussy, manly style—heavy wood, leather, autumnal colours, bottle green and so on. Saskia sat at her father's desk, in her father's swivel chair, a designer piece ordered from Denmark back in the seventies. Black leather and steel. Jenny had confided in Saskia that it was the only good piece her father had ever bought by himself, for himself, and if she were ever to redo his office she would remove everything but the chair and build out from it.

"When they die, it's mine," Jenny said. "You can have the rest of their crap."

Saskia spun the chair in slow circles, propelling herself with a socked foot on his desk drawer, the way she had done all her life. It was raining quietly. In a little while she might pour herself a drink and light the gas fireplace in the sitting room and try the photos again.

The room that was briefly Jenny's had been stripped and redone—new paint, and pale wood flooring where before there had been pale carpet. The hospital bed and the monitors were gone, of course. The room was bare but for a mirrored wall and barre, a green yoga mat, a green Swiss ball, and a CD player on the floor. Saskia pressed play and listened to the beginning of a guided meditation. She pressed stop.

Her parents' bedroom was unchanged, except that the framed family photos were gone. Her mother's chic silk jersey dresses still hung on the left side of the closet, her father's pinstriped suits on the right. In their bathroom, Saskia uncapped and sniffed her father's vetiver shaving cream. She sprayed her mother's Chanel onto one wrist and went through the bathroom drawers, slowly, looking at hairbrushes and prescription tubes of eczema cream (her father) and facecloths and manicure scissors and blood pressure pills (her father) and dry shampoo (her mother, for days when she was too hungover to shower). They had kept their frailties neatly in bathroom drawers, like the old people they were.

Back downstairs, she opened the fridge and studied the condiments: grainy mustard, Major Grey's chutney, lemon curd, butter, Maalox, mayonnaise. Tonic water, but no milk or fruits or vegetables. But of course they had gone on holiday and her mother would have given these to a neighbour before they left. In the freezer were ice cube trays, blueberries, coffee beans, and a couple of small steaks wrapped in butcher paper. Saskia left these on the counter to thaw.

The mail was piled on the island. Her mother would have given the key to a neighbour and asked for it to be brought in, and the plants watered. Saskia would have to retrieve that key tomorrow. Bills, flyers, a newsletter from the Law Society, and a postcard from their old friends the Shaws, who were also vacationing, in Chiang Mai. The Shaws were having a wonderful time. The phone bill included a reminder that their three-year family plan was coming to an end. The Law Society was hosting its annual colloquium on legal aid.

The radio was tuned to the CBC. The television was tuned to the CBC. Their "recently watched" list on Netflix included a travel documentary about Scotland, a documentary about Churchill, *Shakespeare in Love*, the original British *House of Cards*, and *Planet Earth: From Pole to Pole*. They only got ten minutes into that one.

She was aware that she was making lists, probably

some kind of anticipatory defence mechanism. There would be a lot of lists in the days to come.

The closed basement door, just off the kitchen, stared at her.

The wine was kept in the kitchen, the liquor in the sideboard in her father's office. Saskia poured a gin and tonic and found some water crackers in the cupboard to have later with the steaks. But she left the drink on the kitchen counter when she went downstairs because she was not her mother. She didn't need to dull anything.

They had clearly not been down here since Saskia left home. There was a coating of dust on everything, like volcanic ash, and a musty, unaired smell. The door to her old room was open, but Jenny's was still closed. She stripped her old bed, sending clouds of dust skirling into the air, stuffed the linens into the suite's washing machine, and hit start. The machine's measured thump was reassuring. A plate and mug sat atop the TV. Whatever residue remained in the mug had long since transposed into a dense white cobweb of mold. Saskia took the dishes up to the kitchen sink and came back down. She opened a window to the cool, rainy night air.

They had wiped Jenny away upstairs. What had they done down here?

Saskia opened Jenny's door and stood for a while leaning on the doorjamb. Nothing. They had done nothing, touched nothing, removed nothing that Saskia could see. The same dust was everywhere. Her bed was made, her closet was full, her laptop sat closed on her desk.

Saskia imagined herself as Jenny hearing the news of their parents' death. No tears came. From a hook in the closet Saskia took one of Jenny's scarves, a frothy pink thing of some tremblingly fine wool, and buried her face in it.

Upstairs, the phone rang. Saskia added a bullet point to her mental list: *check phone messages.* Then her cell rang in her pocket: Marcel, checking on her. That was kind. She answered so he wouldn't come back to the house, and so he could hear that she had been almost crying. *Doing the things,* Saskia thought. *Doing the healthy grieving things.*

His voice was warm and rough with emotion. So he at least had been crying. They arranged to meet in the morning. He would pick her up at the house and accompany her through the day. He had already been in touch with the authorities in Edinburgh. They would have to visit the consulate for paperwork, call the airline, arrange a funeral home to receive the remains, and so on. There would be phone calls to make, informing people, but he said Christine would do those. Saskia was not alone, he stressed. They loved her like a daughter, and would be with her every step of the way. He probably meant it too.

After promising him she'd try to get some sleep, Saskia turned her phone off. She decided to spend the night in Jenny's room. She moved around the house—making up Jenny's bed, shifting the laundry to the dryer, pouring the gin down the sink, frying and eating the steaks, unpacking her overnight bag and getting into her pyjamas—while grief broke over her in waves. Far between, at first, and then closer and closer together, like labour pains, or (eventually) a heartbeat. Finally she went into Jenny's room and got under the covers, but the thump of the dryer was overwhelming. It was so much louder in Jenny's room than her own, and she thought about all the times she had set a load to run just before going to bed, and Jenny had said nothing. She got up to close the door.

Hanging on a hook on the back of the door was a black leather dog collar and leash. Someone had Sharpied *remember what you are* on the door with an arrow pointing to the collar. Someone not Jenny. It wasn't her handwriting.

"Does your family have a dog?" the young woman named Madhu asked two days later.

"No, never. My mother was allergic."

"And you don't recognize the handwriting? No one in your family?"

Her father's square printing, her mother's scrawl, Jenny's cheerful loops. "No."

The young woman looked at the photo on Saskia's phone again. "Does it mean anything at all to you? Remind you of anything? Even something that might seem irrelevant."

Saskia shook her head.

"Looks like she wasn't really trying to hide it."

"I don't know. She always left her bedroom door open, and it was on the back of the door. There's no reason why anyone but her would have seen it."

"You're sure no one's been in her room since the accident? Two years is an awfully long time."

"It was so dusty, so unchanged—I think my parents couldn't bear to, and I left home." To this Madhu bowed her head in tactful acknowledgment. "Does it mean anything to *you?*" Saskia asked.

Madhu kept her face blank. "Pretty standard BDSM gear. Was your sister into—"

"No."

"You're sure?"

"No." Saskia touched her temple. "I mean, I guess I'm not sure, no."

"We can look into it." Madhu touched the dog collar and leash, which Saskia had brought in a Ziploc bag. It sat on the table between them. "Where this might have been purchased. Clubs she might have gone to, that kind of thing. Depending on how far you want to take this, we could take a look at her room. Her laptop, her phone. You have those?"

"The laptop is on her desk but her phone got mislaid. I don't know where it is."

Madhu hesitated. "You could also just let this go. It might not mean anything much and it doesn't change who your sister was to you."

Saskia looked around the office, a Yaletown loft with exposed brick walls, pipes running artfully along the ceiling. They sat in low chairs with a Plexiglas table between them. Across the loft sat a couple of young men at another such table, busy on their laptops, occasionally glancing over at them. Her colleagues, Saskia guessed. They were a living TV show, three millennials running an investigative agency, and today's client was the woman with the dead twin who had sexual secrets. Fun!

"I'd like to know who wrote that on her door," Saskia said. "I'd like to know who thought she was a *what* and not a *who*."

Again, that carefully blank face. "Again, kind of standard BDSM . . ." Madhu searched for the word. "Role-play."

"Role-play," Saskia repeated.

———

Marcel Bouchard was as good as his word and guided her through every step. The funeral was expensive. Her parents' trip to Scotland was expensive. Shelby, her mother's clinic, was very expensive. The house was worth a lot of money, but they had used retirement money on their abortive attempt to bring Jenny home, and then on all the lawsuits her father had launched and lost after that. Still, there was enough in the estate that Saskia wouldn't have to work for a few years, if she was frugal. She might not even have to sell the house right away.

"Though maybe better to get it done, no?" Marcel suggested. "A fresh start?"

"Not yet." Saskia hadn't told him about what she had found in Jenny's room. She was sitting at the kitchen table with her sheaves of lists in front of her, talking to him on the phone. She had given notice at the coffee shop. Next on her list was to cancel the lease on her crappy apartment and move her few belongings back here. She would drop her student furniture at the Sally Ann on the way.

The doorbell rang. "I have to go," she told him. "There's someone at the door. More flowers, probably."

"*Nous t'aimons,* Saskia." It had become his sign-off. We love you.

Downstairs, she opened the door to Madhu and her colleague, whom she introduced as Jay. Jay held up an iPad, where he had written *nice house!* He grinned widely at her.

"Jay is deaf," Madhu said. "He reads lips."

"Nice to meet you," Saskia said.

Nice to meet you too!

Saskia led them to the door to the basement suite. "Down here."

"Could we see the whole house after?" Madhu asked. "I mean, if it's okay. You never know."

Jay nodded vigorously.

"Sure, I guess," Saskia said.

In Jenny's room they were methodical, going through drawers and closets, putting everything back neatly as it was. Maybe they really had done this before. *May I?* Jay wrote, pointing at Jenny's laptop.

Saskia took Madhu around the rest of the house while he sat with Jenny's computer. "Jay's my cousin," Madhu said. "He's really thorough, especially on the tech side."

"Have you had cases like this before?"

Madhu looked through her parents' bedroom window into the backyard. She turned back, her eyes roving up and down, but unlike in Jenny's room she didn't open any drawers. "Not exactly. No two cases are exactly alike."

"But some parts are?"

Saskia saw her choosing her words. "We get a lot of sexual behaviours," she said finally. "Lot of adultery. Lot of questions after a person has died and their pay-per-view statement comes and there's all that porn or whatnot. Lot of figuring out after the fact that someone spent their life in the closet. Loved ones don't always like what we have to tell them."

"Do you ever not tell them?"

"Sometimes." Madhu peered into her parents' closet. "If someone might get hurt. I mean really hurt, like revenge. Some secrets are nobody's business."

"So if you don't take my money, I'll know there's something you're not telling me?"

"Oh, we'll take your money," Madhu said.

When they got back downstairs they found Jay at the kitchen table with Jenny's laptop. He signed something to Madhu. "He wants to look for your sister's phone," she said.

They all went back downstairs to Jenny's room again and Saskia retrieved the purse, Jenny's camel suede Longchamp that she had spent an entire paycheque on, from the closet. She dumped the contents out on the bed. Wallet, makeup, keys, tissues, a travel tube of ibuprofen, and nail polish in the sky blue Jenny had been wearing at the time of the accident.

"Maybe your parents put it somewhere for safekeeping?" Madhu said.

In-home safe? Jay wrote. *Bank safe deposit box?*

Briefly, Saskia wondered if this was all a ruse for them to rob her. She shook her head. "I would have found it in those places already."

"What about the find-my-phone app?" Madhu asked.

Saskia shook her head. "She disabled it. She hated the idea of being tracked."

Try calling it? Jay suggested.

So Saskia called Jenny's phone number, and they all listened in case it rang somewhere in the house, but it went straight to message. Jay slapped his forehead and grimaced at his cousin, because of course the battery would have died long ago. Saskia listened to her twin tell her to leave a message and she would get back to her.

Saskia took to calling her sister throughout the day, just to hear her recorded voice. Of course her parents hadn't cancelled Jenny's phone, couldn't bear to. These voicemails studded her days, like pills or cigarettes. She'd pull her phone out whenever she had a moment, or whenever she felt her chest tighten. *I'll get back to you.*

Saskia also searched the house relentlessly, soon ritually, but the phone never surfaced. She contacted the cell phone company and got a log of her sister's calls and texts, but they only showed the times they were made, not the content. She searched her sister's room inch by inch: prising up the vent grills, shining a flashlight under the bed, unzipping the mattress cover, going through all the pockets in her clothes. Nothing.

She debated painting over the Sharpie on the back of the door. The words changed inflection almost every time she looked at them. They were sinister that first night, soiling her sister's memory. They had less power in sunlight. Sometimes they almost seemed affectionate. Dogs had many admirable qualities, didn't they? Loyalty, and so on? At times Saskia even allowed herself to contemplate the obvious: that her sister had had a sex life she kept secret, had tastes she knew her twin would neither share nor understand. Her sister was into role-play, BDSM. So what?

I don't understand, that's what, Saskia thought. *I've had to understand so much, all my life. Be understanding.* She thought of the times she tried to explain to Joel what it was like. *It sounds lonely,* he said once, which made her laugh. It was the opposite of lonely. Jenny was her sun and moon: there was no escaping her. Saskia was ever alert to the ways her sister could hurt her, ever afraid of the ways Jenny might hurt herself. She had quoted

Archilochus back at Joel: *A fox knows many things, but a hedgehog one important thing.* Saskia knew Jenny. She'd suffered that knowledge all her life. Jenny didn't get to have secrets now just because she was dead.

In the local paper she looked at the personal ads. She searched for clubs online and found many. She thought about visiting one, but she wanted only to see what her sister had actually seen, know what her sister had known. Since she didn't know which clubs or fetish nights Jenny might have frequented, Saskia stayed home.

She dialled her sister's number again and again. She listened to her sister's voice.

Within a few days, her research into the BDSM world had begun to bore her. She remained doggedly unaroused by it all, the leather and whips and clips and so on. On one of the club websites she'd found: *Please wipe down dungeon equipment with disinfectant provided!* On another: *Let's play it safe, sane, and consensual!* Her own tastes were mainstream and perfunctory. She never had difficulty masturbating, or took long. With Joel she had rubbed her breasts in his face and then assumed the missionary position. He had wanted to be gentle because she was grieving, and because he was essentially a gentle man. Not long after the funeral he told her he'd been accepted into a graduate program in International Policy at Stanford. Saskia told herself she didn't care. After all, she'd won Jenny's ten-dollar bet. She didn't need him anymore.

Christine Bouchard cooked cassoulet with a big green salad. For dessert was tarte Tatin served straight from her cast-iron frying pan. It was the first time since the funeral that Saskia had agreed to a meal at their house, though they'd asked many times. "Oh my goodness, Christine," Saskia said, as they took their coffee cups to the living room. "That was amazing."

"You come live with us and I'll feed you every day of the week. Now that my nieces and nephews are grown, I only have Marcel to spoil. It's not enough."

"Her heart is too big," Marcel said affectionately.

And yet, Saskia reflected, Christine had never come to see Jenny after the accident, neither in the hospital nor at their home. She knew what Jenny was.

What, but not *who,* Saskia thought. She didn't need mothering from Christine.

"I'll keep asking until you say yes," Christine was saying. Saskia smiled and said how appreciative she was, but that she wasn't ready to leave her parents' house.

They chatted for a while about a TV series they had both enjoyed, a Swedish thriller. While Marcel puttered about tidying the kitchen, Christine loaned her a collection of poetry in French by a Senegalese writer. "Do you ever think about resuming your studies?"

Saskia shook her head. "I've had trouble reading since Jenny died. I watch TV instead." The slim volume in her hands had a worn cover, cardboard showing through the threadbare green fabric, and looked quite old. Saskia guessed it was one of Christine's treasures, and her mind flickered briefly to Professor Taillac and the book he had given her. "I'll enjoy this, though," she said quickly.

Christine laughed. "There's no shame in watching TV! I just thought you might ease back in with some poetry. Just a little at a time, a page every now and then. Your parents always imagined you teaching at a university one day."

"They wanted me to have status. They wanted to be able to brag about one of us to their friends."

Christine leaned forward. "And why not? Parents want to be proud of their children. They want to see them succeed and make fine lives for themselves. And, yes, they want to brag to their friends. If that's all you have to hold against your parents, you're lucky."

Saskia now realized that Marcel had been instructed to remain in the kitchen while Christine had a chat with her. They were going to get to the heart of something, now, here tonight. Fun!

"You're angry, *petite puce*. You try so hard to hide it

because you're polite and well brought up. But don't you think it might feel good to talk to someone about— everything? All that you've suffered, all that you've lost?"

"A psychiatrist?"

"A counsellor. Someone to guide you, a little. Not too much. I don't think Saskia is ever one to be guided too much." She smiled.

Saskia took a deep breath. "Of course, you're right. I should work through—everything. With someone."

"Anger is okay. But letting go is okay too. And so is agreeing with me so I'll change the subject."

Saskia laughed dutifully, and Christine laughed, too, and Marcel took this as a signal to return to the living room. He offered cognac with the coffee, but Saskia and Christine both refused and he left the bottle on the table without opening it. Tomorrow was a workday for him and it was getting late. Saskia rose and thanked them for the supper, and the company. Christine invited her to brunch on Christmas Eve, two weeks hence, and she couldn't quickly think of an out. Would eleven work? They all three pulled out their phones.

"What is this update?" Marcel asked Christine, squinting at his phone. "Do I need to do this right now? Where are my glasses?"

"Useless, I tell you," Christine said to Saskia. It was unclear whether she meant the update or the man.

Saskia took a few steps back into the hall and dialled her sister's number, almost automatically, as she waited for the couple to figure out how to access Marcel's calendar. It rang.

It rang.

Christine looked up first, and met Saskia's gaze. Saskia held her phone away from her ear, listening to her sister's phone ringing somewhere in the house. Then it went to message.

Now Marcel was looking at her too. She dialled again. The phone rang again.

"Where is it?" Saskia asked.

Marcel's home office, it turned out, was just off the foyer. Jenny's phone was in Marcel Bouchard's briefcase, in Marcel Bouchard's office, in Marcel Bouchard's home.

"I can explain," Marcel Bouchard said, just as Christine said, "We can explain."

Then they were sitting in the living room again with the phone on the coffee table between them. Marcel reached for the cognac but Christine touched his wrist. Saskia felt cold.

Marcel said, "After the accident I went with your father to the police station to reclaim her effects. Her—things."

Effects, Saskia thought, analyzing automatically. The effects one left on the world once one was gone. The ripples as one sank. A word from the book of the dead, *effects.*

"They gave your father everything in a clear plastic bag. He became . . . emotional, and went to the washroom. He left the bag sitting on the chair next to mine in the lobby."

Her father crying silently in a washroom cubicle as the uniforms came and went. Saskia could picture it. "The lobby of the police station," she repeated when Marcel paused to make sure she was hearing him. He knew her moods well enough, knew her numbness, her withdrawal, her grief, her rage. Her hot-and-sour soup of those.

"The phone rang. In the bag. I saw the screen light up. I saw . . ." He looked at Christine, who made a minute movement of her head, almost as though she needed to stretch her neck. Saskia read distaste. "I saw something your father didn't need to see," he said. "I didn't really think. I just put it in my pocket."

"We looked and looked for it," Saskia said. "We took the house apart trying to find it. He thought he was losing his mind."

Marcel looked at his hands. "I put the phone in a drawer at work and tried to forget about it. It rang sometimes." He looked guardedly at Saskia, and she knew how often he must have seen her name light up the screen. "I brought it home tonight because you were coming, but Christine was worried you weren't ready."

Saskia reached for the phone. They didn't try to stop her, but Christine said, "You don't have to, *petite puce*. Let us carry this one for you."

"What could be so terrible?" Saskia looked from her sister's phone to her parents' friends and back. Rose-gold, with a nick in one corner she had forgotten she knew. She might never have thought of it again, that nick, and that would have been another fragment of her sister lost. "What could be so terrible that you would steal from us?"

They said nothing. Shame and sadness made them children, heads bowed before her anger. "You were a judge," she said to Christine.

Christine lifted her chin and met Saskia's gaze. "Look, then," she said.

But Saskia put the phone in her bag and stood up. It would have something to do with the dog collar, of course. "My sister had a private life. You think I didn't know? A private life that wasn't yours to police. Or disapprove of. Or—*judge*—in any way." She leaned punishingly on the word. "You think I didn't know?"

Christine looked down. Her father's colleague put his hand over his eyes.

At the door, Saskia turned to Marcel one last time.

"You've had this phone for almost two years. How is it still charged?"

"What?" Christine asked.

"The battery would have died long ago. You charged it."

Christine turned to her husband with incomprehension. He said nothing.

"You looked at it every once in a while." It was one of those rare moments in life when thought and speech walked perfectly in step, neither preceding the other. Saskia indicated Christine with her chin. "*She* didn't. But you did."

She left them there: pride and prejudice, sense and sensibility, horror and humiliation. She would never see them again.

She got in her car and drove to a neighbourhood she had never been to before and would probably never return to. She parked on a quiet street and pulled the phone from her bag. Of course she knew Jenny's password, as Jenny had known hers. Twins, after all.

The photos were more or less as she had expected, whips and gags and so on. The accompanying texts were terse: *Don't be late. You loved this. You bruise easy.* Moments before the accident, with no photo and no context: *Right now, I dare you.* After that were more pictures, what Marcel must have seen in the lobby of the police station.

Skipping work, drinking and driving, speeding through a red. It could have been any of these, all of these. Jenny had never been one to refuse a dare.

Saskia clicked to Contacts and stared at the name of the man who had sent the last text Jenny ever read, who had taken those photos and caused Jenny so much pain (obviously) and even, perhaps, some hellish pleasure. Robert Dwyer.

CHAPTER EIGHT

January 2018

Saskia learned of the death of Mattie Landow from Google. She had been searching Robert Dwyer's name, trying to summon the courage to contact him directly. She clicked on an article from two summers ago, eight months after Jenny died: *Addict implicated in death of developmentally disabled woman.* The funeral, she learned, had been held at the Anglican church in her parents' neighbourhood. Mattie Landow was survived by an elder sister, Sara Landow, a UBC professor.

The professor's contact info was on the website for the UBC Centre for Applied Ethics, an interdisciplinary program that brought together philosophers, nurses, sustainability experts, lawyers, journalists, and geneticists. Her bio listed her expertise as medical ethics. Her most recent published paper was on capacity and consent in adults with special needs. The accompany-

ing photo showed a plain woman in her early forties,
Saskia guessed, with fine, dirty blonde hair pulled back.
She wore a black sweater that looked soft, even on the
computer screen, and a pendant on a chain so fine it was
almost invisible.

After considerable deliberation—call every Landow
in the phone book to find her at home? make an appointment during her office hours?—Saskia decided to email
her work address. She received an automated response
letting her know that Professor Landow was away from
the University on a personal matter and would reply
upon her return. There was nothing to do now but wait.

A week after she reached out, she received a brief
email from Sara Landow, asking if she was free to meet
at a coffee shop on Granville Street, downtown.

In person, Sara Landow was less poised than her
photo had suggested. She looked both puffy and haggard
in a way that was viscerally familiar to Saskia. A drinker,
then. They shook hands.

"I'm sorry about your sister."

Sara Landow inclined her head, accepting the con-
dolence. "You said in your email you had information
about—him. If it's regarding a criminal matter, you
should give it to the police."

"But here you are."

What must she look like to this professor of applied

ethics, in her expensive trench coat and glossy boots? A graduate student, probably, frozen in time two years after she had ceased to be a graduate student. Jeans and a blue rain jacket from MEC, Vancouver camo. She chewed not her nails but the skin around them, leaving the cuticles scabbed.

"I had a sister. Her name was Jenny. She died too. But you wouldn't have heard about it on the news."

"I'm sorry."

Sara Landow stared at the table between them as Saskia related the story of her twin's car accident and subsequent medical condition. She raised her eyes when Saskia told her about that last text.

"It doesn't sound like the same man," Sara said when Jenny was dead and Saskia was finished speaking.

Of all the things she might have said, Saskia had not anticipated this. She blinked.

Sara touched her fingertips to her temples. "I'm sorry," she said again. "What do you want? From me?"

"Whatever that last text meant, whatever the dare was, it caused Jenny's accident. The police might not have put it together, but I know. He only got a year in your sister's case. He got nothing for mine. It's not enough."

"What do you do for a living?"

Saskia waved this away. "It's not enough," she said again.

"I agree." Sara touched her fingertips to the table-top near Saskia's hand. "I'm sorry for all you've been through, Saskia. But I don't think I can help you. It's a legal matter, surely."

"Aren't you angry?"

At this Sara started pulling on her gloves. Her black butter leather gloves. Saskia felt a flare of hatred for the older woman. "Why did you say it didn't sound like the same man?"

"Right now, I can't imagine a day in my life when I don't think about him. When I don't wonder what I might have done differently, and how much I'm to blame. I want to move on. I need to move on." Sara stood. "I'm very sorry for your loss." She left the coffee shop.

Saskia lifted her mug, put it down again. The woman is grieving, she reminded herself. It's too soon, that's all.

She caught up to Sara across the street, where she was waiting for a bus. "Why don't you think it's the same man?"

"He never hurt my sister. That way." The bus came. "Please don't contact me again."

"You have my email," Saskia called after her as she boarded. "If you change your mind."

CHAPTER NINE

Spring 2018

After meeting Saskia, Sara quit drinking. David Park approved. He told her his wife, a senior administrator with the City of Vancouver who was also a major fundraiser for the hospital where David worked, wanted to put on a concert to buy the hospital some piece of equipment for the children's wing. He remained a spectacular amateur violinist, and wanted Sara to accompany him. He said practicing again would give her something healthy to focus on.

"No. I haven't played in years."

"It's like riding a bike."

David outlined the program he'd already chosen: Bach, Beethoven, and a forbidding contemporary work excreted by the Dutch composer Claes deWinter. Sara knew he had folded his heart inside that last one.

She scanned the score, which he had brought with

him to coffee. It was too big for the tiny round table, and too loud in the Granville Street café for her to hear it properly in her head. Still. "It's awful. You know I hate prepared piano. It's stupid."

"It's just corks."

"Wedged into the strings." She shook her head. "Piano rape."

"Don't knock it till you try it." David flashed the grin that had raised his hospital millions over the years.

"What does Alice think?"

Petite, lovely Alice, whose parents were in the Communist Party stratosphere back in Beijing, who carpooled to yoga with the mayor's wife, who was raising their children without animal proteins or television. "She thinks she can get Claes over for the performance."

"Claes?"

"We met him at that conference last year, in Bern."

"Who *don't* you know?" Sara turned a page of the score. "I thought Alice told you to stay away from me."

"She knows it's over."

Sara didn't know, but pretended not to react.

"Please, Sara. It'll be good for both of us."

"I'll need at least six months."

"You'll have eight. I'm thinking November. The University will donate performance space in the Chan Centre. We'll have the summer to rehearse."

She gave herself over to the sensations of the coffee shop to still her thinking for a moment. She opened herself to consciousness of the uneven wood floor, the chocolate-smoke smell of the coffee, the hiss of the machines and the voices raised over them, even the humidity on her skin from the hot-milk steam, the many bodies and their furled wet umbrellas in this overheated space. The image of a glass of Malbec came. She allowed it, considered it, and turned away from it. She had been doing this for a few weeks now, and was careful never to let herself think it was something she was good at. She had to decide every time as though for the first time.

"I thought you'd be pleased." David tapped the score. "At the coincidence."

Sara looked at him.

"DeWinter," David said.

Sara looked at her hands.

"Do you still have it?"

The image of the glass returned, bashful, fetching. She allowed it, considered it, turned it away. "No."

"Liar."

"Yes, I still have it. It's in storage." She closed the score and put it in her bag. "I'll call you when I'm ready to start rehearsals."

———

Sara had gotten rid of her mother's piano when she sold the Kerrisdale house. There was no room for it in the apartment and she wouldn't have been allowed to play it at any rate because of the noise bylaws. She wouldn't have wanted to play it. But now she needed to practice, so she went to Long & McQuade on Terminal Avenue and bought a keyboard with headphones. It had weighted keys to imitate the action of a real piano, and was so compact she took it home that same day in a taxi van. The thing was violently expensive, but Sara had money. While they fetched it from the stockroom, she browsed the sheet music and added a Hanon exercise book, the complete Beethoven sonatas, and several volumes of Bach to her purchase. She hesitated over the Romantic and twentieth-century repertoires, but found in herself no emotional traction there. No longer, or not today.

She turned Mattie's old bedroom into a music room. Though she and David had cleared the room out together a year ago, she had never comfortably repurposed it and tended to throw things in there without much thought. The rest of the apartment was spare and stylish, but that room was a jumble. She called another taxi van and took a load to the Sally Ann, and then there was room to set up the keyboard. She filled the bookcase that used to hold Mattie's movies with scores and CDs.

On another excursion she had found a CD of a different deWinter, an orchestral work. She didn't listen to it for a long time but often looked at the cover, an unremarkable white and grey abstract painting, with the composer's name and the title of the work, *Grijs Licht*, in unobtrusive type. There was something so clichéd about it—the dull painting, the tasteful font, the title, which translated as "Grey Light"—that it made her want to giggle. As though it had been decided by a committee in a corporate boardroom somewhere. Or in a university—that would be it—by achingly clever people making pronouncements to each other about Sound Art.

She tired quickly during her first few days of practice, and her old weaknesses reappeared immediately: the tightly cocked fifth fingers and the consequently aching elbows, early signs of tendonitis. She slowed down and spent a couple of weeks on scales and Hanons, forcing herself to relax her jaw. She had a tendency to clench her teeth when she was concentrating, which tightened everything in a downward domino trail. She practiced with the propped CD on the stand in front of her. Smiling unknotted her fifth fingers.

David had chosen Bach's first sonata for violin and harpsichord, BWV 1014.

After three weeks, she phoned him to say it wasn't possible. He laughed.

"No, listen," she said.

They met at the empty loft of a colleague, a neuro-surgeon, who had a concert grand in his penthouse high above Gastown. The colleague was on rotation some-where. The Yukon? The view was of the container port.

She tried. She played. He listened. They played together.

"Huh," he said.

Her replacement would be a UBC music student. "Don't beat yourself up about it," David said. She returned the keyboard for a full refund. So it really was over, except for twice. Once that time in the loft with the view of the container port—that was in March. Once in September. He had been miserable about that second time, she could tell. She understood with a certainty born of absolutely nothing that she had been replaced, but he wasn't ready to admit it. So teeth and nails, tooth and claw, marks for him to have to explain to Alice or whoever.

The concert was in November. Sara made a large dona-tion with her expensive ticket and sat towards the back, but Alice found her anyway.

"There's a reception after, backstage, for Claes. You must come. Is that the dress?"

So David had told her about the dress.

Sara smiled. "No. That would have been mutton dressed as lamb."

Alice beamed at her, and turned to greet other significant donors. She was tiny and electric and smelled of vanilla, orange, and smoke.

Sara read the program. David's bio was lengthy and immodest, likely written by his publicist. How she had laughed when he revealed he had a publicist. How annoyed he had been! His photo was a few years old. Well, they were reaching that age. The undergraduate accompanist had a mass of dark curls and leaned one milk-fed cheek on her open palm, guilelessly.

Once the audience was seated, the CEO of David's hospital gave a short speech thanking the University and the audience for their generous patronage, and extolling the considerable talents of their own Dr. Park and young Ms. Takasz. The lights went down and the two of them walked onstage. The accompanist had pinned back a tress of hair from each temple so the curls would cascade down her back but her face would be visible in profile. She wore a strapless black floor-length gown. David in his dinner jacket acknowledged the applause, then stepped back so she could get to the piano, murmuring something as she passed that made her smile. She sat and smoothed her skirts. They looked at each other, he nodded, and they began to play.

Sara understood within a few bars what the Bach could sound like, was supposed to sound like; that sad beauty was a kind of food. She also understood that David Park and his accompanist were fucking each other senseless as often as they possibly could. Not a message—Sara thought in spite of herself—Bach was often asked to bear. The glass of Malbec appeared. Allow, consider, dismiss. Atoms moved in orbits, as stars did. Somewhere in the cosmos of her heart a particle collapsed into itself, leaving a black hole the size of a pinpoint.

That's enough, Sara told herself.

Her eyes fell on the glossy blue-black head of Alice Park, fifth row centre, unmistakable even from behind. She sat flanked by President Singh—Sarah knew him from five years of campus Heads and Directors meetings—and a tall, silver-haired man Sara didn't recognize. Alice was watching, too, even as Sara was. She was getting it full in the face.

At intermission, Alice again sought out Sara, who was standing—unobtrusively enough, she had thought—in a corner of the lobby, studying a poster board of upcoming events. Rain streamed down the glass wall that separated them from a patch of old growth forest, high above the black November ocean. They were truly at the edge of the world.

The woman would not go away, so Sara congratulated her on the lovely evening, and they hugged again like old friends.

"I wanted to introduce you to Claes, but he's disappeared." Alice put a hand on Sarah's arm and leaned close. "I think he's nervous. He's hiding in the bathroom."

"Maybe it's his prostate."

Alice's laugh tinkled.

Sara smiled. "It's the premiere, isn't it?"

"He's probably helping Zena set up the piano, come to think of it. Stay here, I'll get drinks." She was gone to the bar, not the lineup but the open end where the staff came and went. A word in someone's ear and she was back with two glasses of white wine. "Cheers." They touched glasses. Sara lifted the rim to her lips but didn't drink. *It's acid, it burns.* Alice knew she was an alcoholic.

"Zena," Alice said. "Such a find."

"A wonderful talent. And David's in fine form tonight."

"Isn't he?" Alice sipped again and looked at the room. She waved at someone across the lobby, a cute finger-wiggle and a wrinkle of the nose. "God, I've forgotten his name. Bruce, Bryce, something. He's a vice president at Bank of Montreal. David practiced like a dog for this."

"It's important to him."

Their eyes met.

"Come backstage, after." Alice patted her arm. "Please."

So the tall, silver-haired man next to Alice was Claes deWinter. Sara had seen him fidget during the Beethoven—dig at his scalp with a single fingernail, look at his watch. Now he sat slumped as though dreading what was to come.

Zena Takasz began the piece standing, leaning into the body of the piano to strum the strings from the inside. David played a brief motif on the violin that he manipulated into a loop via a foot pedal hooked to an amplifier. There was some business with corks and a cloth, some muffling, some zizzing sounds, a crescendo as the loops piled on each other, even snatches of Zena vocalizing into what must have been a microphone hidden inside the piano, her head all but invisible to the audience as she whispered and beseeched. The piece was interminable. By the end—met with a standing ovation—David and Zena were both sweating and breathing hard.

"Extraordinary," the woman next to Sara said.

They watched David conduct the composer to his feet. Claes deWinter turned and bowed to the audience. He had a broad smear of a Dutch face and seemed modest. He smiled and raised a hand in acknowledgement, then quickly resumed his seat.

Hardly had the ovation stopped when Alice was by her side and leading her upstream, against the departing crowd, to a door by the stage. "I was afraid you'd run away."

"You know me too well. But I'm looking forward to meeting Claes."

"Fuck Claes." Alice smiled brilliantly. "I want you to meet Zena. Your replacement."

Allow, consider, dismiss.

"Alice," Sara said, but they were at the dressing room door.

Inside were champagne and flowers and laughter and too many people and David running a cloth over his violin's strings. Sara took Alice's hand from her arm and went to kiss his cheek. There was a smell coming off the cloth, something sweet that she knew. Rose, something? She stopped his hand to lift the cloth to her face.

"Eau de cologne gets the rosin off," David Park said. "It's the alcohol."

Rose, jasmine, mimosa, leather.

"I told you to get rid of that," Sara said. "It was going to be for Mattie. I told you to get rid of it."

"Here we are." Alice was back with the girl. "Here's our Zena. This is Sara Landow, who I've told you so much about. David's *old* friend."

Zena was young and terrified. David closed his eyes for a long moment, then opened them wearily. But they were in a different story. Their loves and lusts and pains and games were not Sara's, not at this moment. "I told you to get rid of that bottle," she said, loudly enough this time for the people around them to fall silent. "That was Mattie's."

"It's not the same bottle." David looked bewildered. "I bought this three months ago. I've been using this brand to clean the rosin. It's like a good luck charm."

"After that first bottle." Sara was aware of hissing through her teeth, literally hissing. "The one I told you to get rid of. I don't care that you gave your stupid wife the stupid Shalimar. But *that* one—"

Some responsible adult took Zena's elbow and led her away from what was obviously going to be a scene. Claes deWinter stepped into the space she left. He really was absurdly tall and ugly.

"I have the pleasure," he said.

So there were introductions, and then somehow the fire went out. David went to see to Zena, and Alice went, too, and Sara was alone with the brother of the murderer who had given his name to the dress she had had her sister cremated in. She hadn't lied to David. The ashes of the dress were in the urn with the ashes of her sister. She'd given her, at the end, her stark black love.

"Come, Sara," Claes deWinter said. "I like the bar out front better."

They sat at one of the two or three tables set up in a corner of the lobby next to the bar. They were alone. The barman had been wiping down the long counter when they arrived, but he assured them that there was another event going on in the Centre, a showing of student films in the cinema annex, which wouldn't let out for another hour at least. The bar was definitely open.

Claes deWinter ordered a carafe of Bordeaux.

"Did you rescue me or did I rescue you?" Sara asked.

He studied her frankly. "Who is Mattie?"

Sara nodded. "I had a sister who died." She ran a fingertip down the stem of her empty wineglass. "The perfume was a gift I had bought for her birthday but hadn't had a chance to give to her yet. After her death, I didn't know what to do with it. I asked David to get rid of it for me."

"Ah."

The wine came. The barman poured two glasses and withdrew.

"Proost," Claes said.

"I was having an affair with David at the time. Alice knew, almost from the start, I think. Tonight was supposed to be her revenge. Because David's sleeping with his pianist now. I didn't know until tonight. She wanted to hurt me with it."

"Honestly, this is not my picture of Canadians. But it's all very exciting. How did your sister die?"

"It was ruled an accident. She fell and hit her head."

"That is too sad." Claes nodded. "And yet I would say sometimes death is preferable. My brother Paul is at La Santé in Paris. You know La Santé?"

"The prison."

Claes nodded.

"Your brother, the photographer. He's still alive?"

Claes made an elegant gesture, *evidently.* "You know his story?"

Sara sipped her wine. "I do."

Sara sipped her wine. Just like that.

"I had the dress for a while. *La petite noire.* I was never brave enough to wear it in public, though Mattie did once."

"Three or four times a year I travel from Rotterdam to Paris to visit him. I take the train and make a weekend of it. I see a concert, go to a museum, buy some clothes, visit my little brother. Drugs were his downfall, but he is clean now."

"Your English is excellent." Sara sipped again. She wondered if Robert was clean now.

"I never understood my brother's work. Such a talent to waste on what—fashion photography, *Vogue?* He could have gone anywhere, done anything. He might have gone to Indochina as a photojournalist. The war brought opportunities for men like him."

"Did he understand your work?"

He held out the carafe. Sara nodded. He refilled her glass and then his own.

"I taught music history at that time. My specialty was the sixteenth-century Flemish motet. So I would suspect that no, he did not."

"When did you start composing?"

They paused to watch a young couple dart across the lobby towards the cinema annex. A cold swirl of night air eddied after them, and they laughed loudly as the girl shook the rain off her hair. The lobby was silent again when they were gone.

"After Paul's scandal. After my divorce. It had to come out of me somehow, I suppose. I was secretive about it for the longest time. I still find nights like tonight difficult. I expose the most intimate parts of myself to strangers."

"So do the musicians," Sara said wryly.

Claes shook his head. "Art is a hierarchy. Myself, the composer, I go at the top. The musicians are less important."

Sara thought about that.

"How is your brother now?" she asked.

"He has become very spiritual." Claes held up the empty carafe until he caught the barman's eye, then placed it back on the table. "Simple, in a manner of speaking. He is awed by simple things. Sometimes I think he is very holy. Sometimes I think the privations of prison have salted his brain. He asks what I eat for breakfast. Coffee and *pain au chocolat*, I say. *Pain au chocolat!* His eyes go big, like a baby's." Claes makes his eyes go big. "So beautiful! he will say. *Pain au chocolat!*"

"What does *he* eat for breakfast?" Sara was conscious now of having to articulate her words against the effects of the wine.

"Do you know, I have never asked him."

They talked through the next carafe, as the barman served the students who began to emerge from the annex. Soon the lobby was as crowded and noisy as David's dressing room had been, and the carafe was empty, and it was time to leave.

"You mentioned a divorce," Sara said as they rose. "You never remarried?"

"Never. No, you will let me take this and I will give it to Alice." The bill. "It's the least she can do for us, yes?"

They retrieved their coats from the coat check and she let Claes help her into hers. "You have yet to praise my composition," Claes said. "All this time I have been waiting."

"It was lovely."

"You didn't understand it."

Sara shrugged.

"That's fine." He didn't seem unhappy. "I hear things on a different plane from most people. A higher plane I will say, yes? I am a sad old slouching divorced Dutchman, but I have this one gift that no one can take from me. I can reach one finger out of this world and into the next, which is more than most people. That gift makes my life meaningful."

"No, it doesn't," Sara said very softly, but he didn't hear her over the noise of the happy students.

They shook hands and said goodbye. Claes spoke to a red-vested usher, who let him into the now-locked theatre so he could make his way back to the party in his honour that they had abandoned an hour ago. Sara stepped into the raw, rainy night towards one of the taxis idling at the curb. The windshield wipers smoothed the rain from the glass. As she got in, the driver spoke into his earpiece in a language she did not understand before putting the car in gear. She lifted the back of her wrist to her nose for the last breath of the scent she had applied earlier that evening—quiet notes of osmanthus flower and tea. Literally the last breath: by the time she inhaled for a second hit, even that was gone.

No matter. She would have the driver stop on the way home so she could get another bottle of Bordeaux. Her night was not over yet.

CHAPTER TEN

June 2018

The phone rang again. It had been ringing for days. Saskia answered, finally. "Yes."

"Saskia? Saskia Gilbert?"

Saskia waited.

"It's Sara Landow."

They arranged to meet the next afternoon in a hotel bar downtown. Sara was there when Saskia arrived, drinking red wine. Saskia ordered tea. Sara had a tremor. Saskia had a headache. After saying hello, they didn't speak until the waitress had left.

They went for supper at a Cambodian place Saskia knew: spicy soup, plastic booths. The kind of place where you didn't bother to take your jacket off. Student food, hangover food. "You look rough," Sara said softly.

"I don't sleep well."

"Neither do I," Sara said.

They went back to Sara's apartment, up in the sky there in Yaletown, near the library. She had some lovely things. The celadon dish on the console in the front hall where she left her keys and coins. The mid-century teak sofa. The astonishing array of perfumes that she kept like condiments in the door of the fridge. The vials of Zoloft and clonazepam and Seconal on the bedside table, next to the phone dock and the hand cream and the wrist brace and the night guard and the brandy.

They went back to Saskia's parents' house. They looked at photos, and Saskia showed Sara Jenny's clothes, which filled her closet. She'd gotten rid of pretty much everything else.

They arranged to meet at a hotel bar downtown, a different one. Sara knew a lot of these places, expensive and anonymous, where if you were wearing nice clothes you could drink a little too much and no one would remember you.

They went for Lebanese at Cambie and Hastings, across the street from the cenotaph where the drug dealers watched and waited. They argued that time.

The phone rang again. "I'm sorry," Saskia said, and Sara said, "*I'm* sorry."

They went back to Sara's apartment. They agreed about some things, disagreed about others. At times each blamed the other's intransigence on the other's age. So old! So young! So green! So grey! So hard! So soft!

Actually, they were both hard: angry and unforgiving. Actually, they were both soft, tender with pain and childlike with incomprehension.

"Do you ever wonder about consent?" Sara would ask, and Saskia would repeat the things she'd read about safe words and the psychology of the submissive. "But in the car, that text," Sara would say, and Saskia would shrug. What must Jenny have been thinking in that moment?

———

"Do you think Mattie was happy with him?" Saskia asked. Sara looked at the bar; nodded at the bar.

They met for the last time at a pub on Granville Street during happy hour. The place was packed, and they had trouble hearing each other. Not that there was much left to talk about by that point.

Saskia left first. Sara watched her go. She was brittle. A man bumped her and she turned and swore in his face, startling him out of the apologetic grin he had put on. So brittle. Bit by bit she would chip off, shards sharp enough to cut, until there was just a blade of her left in the body's sheath.

Sara left first. Saskia watched her go. She was frail. Her mind would give out, and her liver. That was guilt. It was the difference between them. Guilt would be the death of Sara, but not of Saskia. There she goes, Saskia thought, in her lovely coat, that cashmere-and-guilt blend so few can afford. That lovely perfume she trails, lilies and guilt. At the door Sara turned and looked back at Saskia, as though she had just remembered something she meant to say, and touched her heart. Saskia almost smiled.

They never spoke again.

PART THREE

CHAPTER ELEVEN

December 2018

In winter the ocean turned the colour of iron and the sky went pale when it wasn't raining. Rain smudged the world charcoal. Sara spoke with her doctor and her dean and they agreed to a medical leave. She sat in her reading chair, wrapped in a blanket, sipping her wine and watching the greyscale of sea and sky visible from her living room windows. Every day, she balanced the entire weight of her body on a single toe, *en pointe,* and held it. That was what it felt like. Her psychiatrist said this was delayed grief. Dr. Kumar was a gentle Buddhist who really, really wanted her to quit drinking again and get more exercise.

The phone rang again. She ignored it again.

Hours later, the phone issued the particular stutter of the intercom. Someone was at the front door. This, too, had happened several times. But the next morning,

when she went out for coffee and chocolate and oranges
and bread—her supplies—she found a note stuck under
her nameplate. She tore its little corner, easing it out.
He told her later he'd stood across the street for a long
time that night, watching the light in her window, seeing it go out. He'd stood for a long time after that, waiting. After all, she was the one who had reached out
to him.

Her friend Donna August could not understand any of
it. They stood in Hermès, arguing.

"Petrichor." That was the word Sara had been trying
to remember. The saleswoman beamed. Rain on stone—
petrichor! *Ding-ding-ding-ding-ding!*

"He doesn't deserve your time, even for a coffee,"
Donna August said. That was one of the things Sara had
always intermittently liked about her: she said things
straight, even unspeakable things like this one, which
was clearly about class. "You're sick and you're not
thinking straight."

"You said I wasn't sick." That had been the week
before, when Sara was trying to explain the nature of
her leave and Donna, in her stern and authoritative way,
was denying the existence of clinical depression. "Petrichor and jasmine." Sara nodded at the saleswoman,

who began to wrap the small orange box with a chocolate brown ribbon. *Oranges and chocolate.* "It's just coffee."
Donna snorted.

Her friend instructed the saleswoman to find her a
proper musk, nothing fruity. She excused herself and
they watched her walk to the back of the shop. "You're
vulnerable and he'll take advantage of you. Again. I
don't know why you can't see it."

Sara felt herself tire. It came over her like a tide these
days. "Maybe he's changed."

"Idiot," Donna hissed. They watched the saleswoman
emerge from a discreet door in the back wall and come
back to them with a handful of samples. She wore a
black sheath and, round her neck and tucked into her
belt, an indigo scarf of some impossible fabric, fairy
wings, probably. Ten pounds of fairies to make a single
scarf, harvested at dawn by peasant women in kerchiefs
as the dew began to steam and the field fairies were just
drifting up out of the grip of gravity. The women used
nets. Once pinioned, the little bodies were tossed into
sacks for soup. It was a whole way of life.

"Addiction is a sickness," Donna said. Conversation-
ally. Sara understood this to mean their conversation,
their argument, was to continue in front of the saleswoman. *The help,* Donna would have called her, with and
without irony.

"It is." The saleswoman sprayed a *touche* and gave it to Donna, who gave it to Sara after she had sniffed. Donna accepted a second *touche* but held on to it as she finished her thought. "Have that coffee, and see if he doesn't want something. No, I don't like any of these. What do you want with him, anyway?"

They left the shop, Sara with her little orange bag. Christmas was coming and Robson Street, when they turned onto it, was crowded.

"It's part of the process," Sara said. "Putting the past to rest."

Donna rolled her eyes.

They met at a coffee shop on Hastings Street in Burnaby, near where he was living now. He'd suggested the place on the note he'd left under her nameplate. He had drifted for a while, but now he was back in town, working again and trying to keep clean.

"I have a friend who says you're going to take advantage of me." It had taken Sara an hour on transit to get here from downtown. "Are you?"

"That's cold."

Sara shrugged.

His hand, when she shook it, had been dry and calloused, catching in Sara's memory on the one other time she'd shaken his hand, the day she learned he had married her mentally handicapped sister. (There were other terms that had since gained currency, but Sara was a child of the seventies and "mentally handicapped" was what she had grown up with, what stuck.) David Park's hands had been soft, manicured. Surgeon's hands. The hands of her on-and-off lover. Off, now. Never mind.

Robert Dwyer wore a blue check flannel shirt that suited his dry, off-ginger colouring and his pale blue eyes. He wore jeans and leather shoes, and she saw a black leather jacket over the back of a chair at the table he led her to. Early; he had beaten her. She wondered if that gave him a subtle advantage. Donna would have said this was out of character for a former drug addict, former grifter, former inmate, and would have said it was a sign that he was putting on an act for her. But Sara thought she knew a little more about his character than Donna. He had not, during his brief marriage to her sister, done anything other than try to make her happy. Yes, he had moved into their mother's grand old Kerrisdale mansion with her, slept with her, and spent her money. But he was clean and tidy, cooked good meals, made home repairs, and disappeared without fuss the day Sara came over with a court order.

Arguably it was the drugs that had dictated his return to their lives, but even through that fog he had done his best. When Mattie smashed her head he had known the police would come, but he hadn't run. He had held her. She hadn't died alone.

"Sara." His voice, too, was appealingly dry and husky, years of cigarettes, probably.

"Robert."

Coffee for her, green tea for him. He insisted on paying. *Wrong,* Sara thought at Donna August. *You're wrong about him.*

"How are you?" he asked.

She said nothing, studying him. More lines on the face, more grey in the ginger. But she had not grown any younger herself.

"Plans for Christmas?"

He was mocking her now. Mocking her silence with conversation as though they were some kind of friends.

"I have a friend who says I shouldn't have reached out to you. She says you're going to use this opportunity to take advantage of me. Are you?"

"That's cold."

Sara shrugged, then shivered.

"*You're* cold," he said. "You need a warmer coat."

"I'm going shopping later." She had promised herself a treat for getting through this.

His lips quirked, and she saw he knew it was true. He knew her, in his way. It was odd. "Mattie always said you liked to shop."

Her name between them, a coin on the table. Who would pick it up?

"What can I do for you, Sara?" Robert said.

Sara took a deep breath and exhaled. "I want to visit her grave," she said. "With you."

He sat back, studying her.

"I'm not a Christian," she said. "I don't believe Mattie's watching us. I don't believe any of that. But I miss her and I thought you might miss her too."

He shook his head. "You don't care about that."

"You don't know me."

"No, I don't know you." His face, in that moment, was unreadable. *If he was looking for an advantage,* Sara reasoned with the voice of Donna August, *he'd put on a show. Furrow his brow. Wipe his eyes.*

Maybe, Donna August replied.

"Come with me," she said.

"Why?"

She paused. Hesitated. "I don't know."

He put his head to one side and studied her. He nodded once.

Damn it, said the ghost of Donna August. Sara tried to smile and started to cry.

———

They stood at Mattie's graveside. Her mother had purchased the plot years before. They stood before Sara and Mattie's father's headstone (*Peter James Landow, 1932–1981, Beloved Father and Husband*), and their mother's (*Iris Theresa Lee Landow, 1935–2011 Beloved Wife and Mother*), and Mattie's. *Martha Ellen Landow, 1977–2016* above an etching of a wild rose.

Robert had brought carnations, from Safeway probably, but at least they were pink. Sara had stopped bringing flowers. He had left, or not seen, the price tag on the edge of the cellophane cone: $4.99. Sara was wealthy enough that she rarely bought anything in shops with prices ending in $.99.

"What will yours say?" he asked.

She shrugged.

"The Practical One," Robert suggested.

"The Bitch," Sara offered. Not a word she ever used, for all the feminist reasons, but she suspected it had currency in Robert's idiolect.

"No." Robert touched her shoulder, making her look at him. "I understood. Even at the time, I understood."

He had been quick and sardonic when she first met him. There was something about him now that was slower. That was a change.

They left the cemetery and found another coffee shop. They didn't speak much, but the silence seemed comfortable.

That's how these things start, Sara imagined Donna August saying.

What things?

Donna nodded towards Robert Dwyer, who was studying Sara. He smiled when she caught him, a shy smile. He even coloured a little.

"What?" Sara asked.

"I was trying to see Mattie in you."

Sara nodded. Then she shook her head, looking for the words. "I'm an alcoholic."

He laughed, and after a moment she did too. "You're intense, is what you are. And honest. You don't look much like Mattie, but she was honest too."

"She didn't know how to lie."

"You do, though."

Sara nodded. "You?"

He shrugged, *of course.*

"You look like you've been taking care of yourself since you got out of prison."

He leaned back. "Is that what you want, Sara? You want to hear about prison?"

She got up and went to the counter and bought two toasted everything bagels to go with their coffee. He ate quickly. She was still picking at her first half when he pushed the plate away. "What do you do for work?" she asked.

"Drywall."

She searched for something to say about that. "Where?" she asked finally.

"All over."

"At the moment, I mean."

"Surrey. Did she ever ask about me?"

"No."

"You didn't even have to think about that."

"She didn't. She thought about what was in front of her. You can't take it personally."

"No, I can't take anything personally. I know that. I thought I made her happy, that's all."

"It's like making a dog happy. I'm not sure how much it means by the next day." She touched her temple. "That's an awful thing to say. You must think I'm an awful person."

"I like dogs. I always had dogs when I was a kid."

"Not since then?"

"Not since Mattie."

He was shaming her, or daring her. "Please don't."

He half-turned to get into the coat he had slung over the back of his chair. But then: "I'll show you where I work, if you like."

"In Surrey?"

"It's not so far. Just the one bridge."

"But on transit," Sara said.

It turned out he had come by car, a ten-year-old silver Versa he kept neat and clean.

"I'm not kidnapping you, Sara," he said, as she hesitated with one foot on the lip of the passenger well and one on the sidewalk. "It's just something to do. Have to kill the rest of this day, right?"

It was true. She never knew what to do with herself on grave days, after.

He was a good driver, waving other cars ahead of him and keeping to the speed limit. His work site was a row of half-finished townhouses near a strip mall. It was drizzling, so they parked next to a chainlink fence hung with site safety rules. Beyond the first row of houses was a mud pit. "That's phase two. It's already sold out. Guess what they're worth?"

She shook her head.

"Vancouver is the third most expensive city in the world after Tokyo, Japan, and London, England. These shitholes go for half a million. Half a million for a one-bedroom shithole in the suburbs. You want a burger?"

Sara wasn't sure if things were happening very fast or very slowly. It was genuinely hard to tell.

They made a date for the following weekend and bid goodbye on the sidewalk. He drove off, east, while she went to wait for the SkyTrain, west, back into town. She got off on Granville Street by the Holt Renfrew entrance and found that the ghost of Donna August had been replaced by the ghost of Robert Dwyer. He said nothing but noticed everything, details Sara herself had missed on multiple visits: the Plexiglas sensors at the doors, the padlocked chains looped through the most expensive clothes, the security guards. She showed him a pretty scarf, irises on a watermark of skulls, and told him about the suicide of Alexander McQueen. His rough fingers snagged the silk, or maybe it was her rough thoughts of him.

Sara did not miss her sister, exactly, but there was no one in the world who had been closer to Mattie than Sara, except their mother. Mattie had been work, hard work, and had occupied Sara's mind the way a child would, constantly tugging at her, wanting her attention. Where was she, what was she doing, had she eaten, what had she eaten, was she clean, was she safe, was she bored, was she busy, was she happy? All of this had been Sara's responsibility, and while Mattie was alive Sara had felt resentment. Resentment had transmuted—predictably enough, following Mattie's death—to guilt. But miss her?

In her mind, Sara packed a bag for Paris. She could have gone, could have left the next day. She had time, she had money. In many ways, it was all she wanted. But she feared that some tiny moment would derail her and leave her weeping in some airport departures lounge or Métro car or boulevard—some tiny moment would ruin everything. She had moments of clarity that struck like lightning, or cracking ice. Hairline fractures that revealed the abyss.

And so she packed, again and again, in her mind. The brown boots, suede skirt, grey turtleneck, wool coat, and McQueen scarf for the plane. In her bag the jeans, black cashmere pullover, black dress. Boots with everything. She would buy the rest. *Arrived with nothing; left with a modest number of outrageously expensive clothes.* There was her epitaph.

"I'm an alcoholic," Sara had said. She knew he had once attended NA meetings and had given him an opening, but he hadn't taken it. He assumed intimacy without offering intimacy. An uncluttered approach, anyway.

Sara had a glass of wine while he ate a burger and fries in a sports pub. In the Dairy Queen next door she had coffee while he had ice cream. By the time he dropped her off it was dark. As he pulled up to a red light, she got out almost before the car had stopped, to spare them both the awkwardness of parting. They had already arranged to meet at Mattie's grave again the following weekend, but a bit later in the day.

The next time she saw Donna August she prepared herself for a storm, but her friend was preoccupied with a plagiarism saga involving one of her colleagues at the Law School and didn't even ask about her coffee with Robert Dwyer. Sara realized that for all Donna's imperious judgments about her life, she actually occupied relatively little space in the older woman's mind. Sara said nothing about that meeting, or the next, or the next, and when Donna August finally got around to asking about "that coffee" with Robert Dwyer, Sara was able to say with a degree of honesty, "That was two months ago."

"Did he ask for anything?" Donna asked.

"Money."

Donna August nodded.

He did not, in fact, want money, or at least he never asked for it. She gave it to him of her own accord. She paid for things—meals and parking. He would protest, and then after a while he stopped. He let her pay at the gas station, and once just before parting ways they stopped in at the liquor store beneath the SkyTrain station and he put his two-four of beer right beside her

Côtes du Rhône like they were a couple. That was the day they hugged goodbye, briefly. "Take care, Sara," he said. It was what he always said.

Mattie was in that hug, right there in the middle of it, beaming. Her two best people were friends now.

She asked him how it had happened with Mattie.

"I'd been working around the neighbourhood for a year or so. I'd worked for a roofing company for a summer and we did a job down the street from your mother's house. The homeowner saw I was a hard worker and asked if I could do a few more jobs for him, windows and gutters, yard work, like that. He recommended me to some neighbours, including your mother. I liked her well enough. She was fussy but she paid on time. She used to send Mattie out with coffee and sandwiches. She'd watch us from the front window. I'd tell Mattie sandwiches were my favourite food, or tease her about how pretty she was, and she'd laugh, and then your mother would call her back inside."

Sara nodded. That sounded like her mother: casting Mattie out to the world and then reeling her back in.

"After your mother passed, Mattie was lonely. One night she just asked me to stay. I made her an omelette. I told her jokes and made her laugh. We watched some

TV. I spent a lot of evenings with her when you weren't around."

"You saw an opportunity."

"I saw a lonely girl with too much money and no one getting hurt. I had a dirty life and she was—her face would light up when she saw me. I started looking forward to that."

They had had this same conversation before, or a version of it. But she hadn't believed him then. "Marriage?" she asked, raising an eyebrow.

"I was raised Catholic."

Both eyebrows.

"No, I'm not religious. But she reminded me of being a child. Of being happy and curious and loving people. That was her default setting, loving people."

"You figured that out, did you?"

"Don't be nasty. You weren't around."

"I was around."

"Not in the evening. Not at night."

"Not at night," Sara agreed.

"Nights get lonely. Don't you get lonely, Sara?"

"Settle down," Sara said, and he laughed.

Sometimes he asked the questions. "What was she like as a child?"

"Stubborn. Oh god, so stubborn. She drove us crazy.

She used to refuse to tie her shoes, and my mother refused to help her so she would have to learn, and we spent hours with our shoes and coats on standing around in the front hall, waiting for her to try. Just to try."

"Your mother sounds fierce."

"She knew us too well. She knew our potential, and refused to let Mattie stop short of her potential."

"You too."

"Sure, me too. For me it wasn't oppressive. I was good at school. It was easy for me. I liked to read, I liked to practice the piano."

"Freak. What about your dad?"

"He died when I was ten. Mattie was seven. Heart attack."

"Mattie didn't really remember him. I asked her once and she started to cry. I felt bad."

"Death made her cry. Like a reflex, almost. A learned behaviour, I suppose." She trailed off, thinking about that. Who would she have learned it from? Her mother, as Robert had correctly diagnosed, was fierce. Sara had learned early to keep everything tucked in.

"Hey, Professor. Your dad?"

"He was a journalist. Economic policy, international trade agreements, that kind of thing. He used to travel a lot for the paper and he had a bachelor apartment in Victoria for when the Legislature was sitting. My mother sold it when he died."

"A bachelor pad," Robert said with relish.

"Settle down. He had a law degree from Dalhousie. He started out as a civil servant. Journalism was his second career."

"What was he like?"

"We used to go to Victoria sometimes to visit him, when Mattie and I were little. The place had silverfish and the toilet was always filthy. All he had for furniture was a desk and a typewriter and a TV and a single bed. We had to camp on the floor." Those had been fun times, actually. "He didn't have a kitchen, just a sink and a hot plate. The washroom was down the hall. He shared it, with three other men, I think it was. We used to get deli sandwiches and he and my mother would drink beer from bottles." It was the only time she ever saw her mother drink beer. "I figured that was what adult life was all about, a beer and a sandwich and working to deadline in your own little room. If you leaned out the window you could just see the fairy lights on the Legislature. I hoped that would be my life one day. I knew it wouldn't be Mattie's."

"You still haven't told me what he was like."

"Gentle. Mild. Took his work seriously. Weeks would go by and we wouldn't see him. I assumed that was the way for everyone's dad. When he was home, he was like a visitor in the house."

"Maybe he was a faggot," Robert mused.

"Maybe," Sara said calmly. "We'll never know, now. What about your father?"

"What about him," Robert said, not a question.

Eventually she got more out of him. By this time he was driving her home, and then he was coming up. Not to stay; never to stay. But to drink, and to talk, and to listen. He was the last person in the world who had known Mattie, really known her. Sara sat on the couch with her feet under her. He sat in the reading chair.

"I got my hair from my mother and her mother," he said. "The old lady was born in Scotland, and she knew some words of Gaelic. I have an older sister from a different dad, then me, and then a couple younger brothers. I don't know my brothers. My sister had an aneurysm last year but she's doing okay. We have blood pressure in the family, all of us. Our grandmother raised us for a few years there while our mom went to work up north. She cooked in a logging camp, and when she got home she never wanted to cook. Then my mom married again and I moved out."

"How old were you?" The rain on the window, the fire in the grate, the wine in the cup.

"Seventeen. I took the dog. I loved that dog. A little

bully cross, a rescue. I got an apartment and a job at a gas station. I'd cook us both eggs in the morning and take him for walks in the evening and teach him to be nice around girls. Then my grandmother died. I guess that hit me pretty hard."

Sara read his silence. "Is that when you started using drugs?"

"Well, before then." Robert smiled that crooked half-smile. "But it got worse around then. The dog ran away around the same time."

"I'm sorry. What was his name?"

"Booker."

"Aw," Sara said.

"Because when we first got him, every time he heard a male voice, he would book it. My voice hadn't broken yet so I guess he thought I was a girl."

They built intimacy like this, quietly—embers in the grate, dregs in the cup. After Robert left she would straighten up the apartment and get ready for bed. But she would leave the empty wine bottle on the coffee table until the next morning. Once he left his reading glasses behind. He had taken them out to look at some old photos she had found of Mattie and the family at the beach in Jurassic times, 1978 or so. She didn't mind the wine bottle because she could wash it up and restore it to anonymity whenever she wanted. But the reading glasses were troubling. She found she didn't even want to touch them, so they sat on the table staring at her for the whole week.

"There they are," he said on his next visit, and put them in his pocket. Then she was alone in her apartment again.

After their childhoods, they spoke of their lovers. They each spoke with mature retrospection, and acknowledged each other's evasiveness with only the occasional glance, the half-smile, the sidelong not-quite-look.

Sara spoke without bitterness of David Park, and made the story of the concert into a comedy.

Robert spoke of a woman who was paralyzed in a car accident. This was after Sara had his marriage to Mattie annulled. They had met through friends.

"Friends?"

At a club they both went to, he clarified. He had noticed her there before, but thought she was out of his league. Young, beautiful, confident. One night he asked her to dance, bought her a drink. They chatted. It turned out they had interests in common.

"Interests," Sara repeated.

"Tastes," Robert said. The relationship had developed quickly. She was a thrill-seeker, a risk-taker, like no one he'd ever met before. She was fearless, impetuous, white-hot. He couldn't get enough of her.

"A change from Mattie, then," Sara said.

"I didn't love Mattie," Robert said evenly. "I loved her, though. It got to a point where I couldn't tell if she brought out the best or the worst in me. It didn't matter. I didn't care. I did everything she asked. I did things with her I've never done with anyone else."

"What kind of things?" Sara asked.

"It doesn't matter anymore. She drove away from me one afternoon and the next thing I knew she was in a coma in the hospital. A car accident."

"That's terrible. I'm so sorry."

"I didn't go see her. I couldn't. She'd been so alive, so fierce. I couldn't go see her lying in a hospital bed. I never held her hand again, or kissed her, or told her I loved her. I've never regretted anything so much in my life."

Held her hand. Sara felt a flicker of contempt. "Is that why you stayed with Mattie? When she hit her head?"

He nodded.

Of course it was all heading towards something, and the night finally came in late January, though none of it was as she had expected. She had gone to Mattie's grave as usual but he hadn't showed. She took the bus home and arrived at her apartment wet and cross. She took off her trench coat and the scarf he had once said was pretty. She rubbed her wet hair with a towel and heated up some leftovers for supper. She tried to read.

At a quarter to eight her intercom stuttered. She thought about ignoring it.

When she opened the door, his eyes were wild. She led him to the couch and poured him a brandy, then resumed her place in the reading chair, where she had already spent most of the evening. "What happened?"

His eyes roved her apartment. She saw that he was frightened and that fear made him reckless. He shot the brandy and asked for more. She left the bottle on the table so he could help himself. After a while he took a deep, shaky breath and said, "I saw something."

Sara waited.

"Someone." He barked a laugh. "A ghost."

"Mattie?"

For a moment he looked as though he had no idea who she was talking about. Then he apologized for missing their date at the graveside.

"Who did you see?" Sara asked, but he shook his head. She watched him take another shot of brandy, and another. "Have you eaten?"

Then she was putting crackers on a plate and heat-

ing soup in the microwave. The soup was organic veg-
etable, the second of two cans she had bought months
ago, on sale. She hadn't liked the first one. But she was
lucky to have anything at all for him in the cupboard.
Usually she shopped day by day. She sliced an apple to
go with the crackers and added the last of her salted
chocolate, four squares no bigger than watch faces, indi-
vidually wrapped in rose-gold foil. When she returned
to the living room he had left the sofa and was standing
at the window, staring out at the apartments across the
street. She put the food on the table and went to stand
beside him.

"You stood here once," he said. "And I was down there,
on the sidewalk. And we were talking on the phone. Do
you remember?"

"I remember."

"I was awful to you." He pulled her into a hug and
she let him. He held on until she felt the beginning of
his erection against her leg. He kissed her hair as she
pulled away.

"You should eat before it gets cold," she said.

She remained at the window with her glass of wine
while he ate the soup and the crackers and the apple
and the chocolate. He ate everything and then she said
she had a doctor's appointment in the morning and she
ought to get an early night.

"Are you sure you don't want to tell me any more?" she asked.

He hesitated. "It was nothing. Just the mind playing tricks, you know? I'm really sorry about today. My head was a mess."

She saw him to the door, and then returned to the window to watch him walk down the street a little ways to his parked car. He turned to wave to her, even though she had turned off the living room lights and knew he couldn't see her this time. She didn't wave back.

CHAPTER TWELVE

Spring 2019

Fen, Saskia's realtor, sold the family home for a million over asking. That was Vancouver for you. She took Saskia for bubbles to discuss next steps. That was what she called it: bubbles.

"Something small," Saskia said. "And on a SkyTrain line. I don't want a car."

"Yaletown would be perfect for you," Fen said, but Saskia didn't want to pay a premium to be downtown. She told Fen the suburbs suited her fine. Burnaby, for instance. They arranged to meet in a few days to look at listings. Fen paid for the champagne and put on her black blazer and picked up her black leather valise and Saskia followed her ticking heels to the door. It was raining again. They shook hands, and Saskia stood back under the doorway awning, watching Fen get into her black BMW.

The condo Saskia chose was a studio in an anonymous tower built over a SkyTrain station. You could get to the platform without going outside. The station was on a direct line to downtown—a modest, intelligent, long-term investment. Marcel Bouchard would have approved. The station included a movie theatre and a Safeway and a few hole-in-the-wall places she got to know—the sushi place, the noodle place, the noodle soup place.

On the first night, she got to the building at around four o'clock to receive the keys. She had rented a mini-van for her boxes, and spent an hour hauling them up from the loading zone in front of the building. She stacked them in the front hall, purposely not walking through the rest of the apartment, and went back down-stairs to return the van to the rental place. She took transit back, stopping in for takeout on her way upstairs. She would get groceries tomorrow.

The door clicked closed behind her.

Slowly she stepped from the hall into the main room and savoured the empty newness of the place, the bamboo floors, the stainless fridge, the twenty-third-floor view of the Fraser River. Fen's gift basket—more bubbles, cheese, fruit, chocolate, and an inexplicable stuffed teddy bear—sat on the floor next to the fridge. Saskia put the food in the fridge. She would toss the bear and basket tomorrow. She unrolled her tatami mat and sleeping bag. On the bathroom counter she put her mother's and sister's perfumes. Her father's CDs went on the windowsill: Wagner overtures, the Elgar cello concerto, Bach's *Goldberg Variations*, a Schubert symphony, Strauss's *Vier letzte Lieder*.

Saskia found this music at once dark and luminous, revealing a passionate, melancholic side of her father one wouldn't otherwise have suspected. Sara had laughed when she saw the little collection and called it "greatest hits," which Saskia found condescending. The music was beautiful.

Knives and pots in the kitchen, Jenny's clothes in the closet, laptop and iPhone dock on the floor. She had no way to play her father's CDs, actually; they were only keepsakes. She opened her styrofoam tub of wonton soup and ate on the floor, listening to the overture to *Tristan and Isolde* on YouTube. The night sky was blue and the pinprick lights across the river were orange. The trains were another river, lulling in their regularity, and didn't keep her awake.

The next day, Saskia started wearing Jenny's clothes again. She had recently got her hair dyed dark and glossy and made sure to put on pink lipstick before she went out in the morning and red before she went out in the evening, to the movies mostly. Apart from the clothes, she kept living like a student. Her parents' money sat cozy in its bank account, and she got by on the interest. She liked coming home to her spare little apartment and cooking her spare little meals and watching Netflix on her laptop, or in bed on her phone.

Although she no longer worked, her days were full. She woke early to use the treadmill and free weights in the building's gym. She showered and ate and dressed carefully and took stock of the fridge before she left each morning. She packed a purse with scarf and sunglasses and transit pass and carried a small umbrella. She walked the ten blocks or so north to Robert Dwyer's house and waited across the street until he came out to go to work. She followed him back to the station she lived above, and this was really the trickiest part of the day: following at a sufficient distance that he wouldn't notice her, but then catching up so she wouldn't lose him on the platform. She always tried to get in the next car from his, but once they ended up in the same car and she was terrified he would see her. She kept her sunglasses on and the scarf over her hair and fortunately he gazed out the window the whole time, and never once looked in her direction.

His work site was across the street from a coffee shop.

She could sit there all day, if she felt like it, buying too much coffee and spending enough on lunch that they didn't turf her out for loitering. She couldn't always see him—rarely, in fact—but her view of the main gate meant that she knew where he was at all times. She had a bad moment the first day when a group of workers from the site came into the coffee shop for lunch, but he wasn't with them, and gradually she was able to relax into her days there.

At 4:00 p.m., when he and the others would leave, she would follow at a distance back to the station. Sometimes he would duck into a pub with some of them and she would simply wait across the street until he emerged, rarely more than an hour later. She would tail him home on the train, sometimes following him through Safeway as he bought his Dr Pepper and a dozen eggs, and then back north to his home. He never saw her, she was confident of that. After the door closed behind him she would walk back to the Safeway, buy her own provisions, and go upstairs to her evening.

Those were weekdays. Weekends he rarely emerged from the house, except on Sunday afternoons. Then she would follow him to Mountain View Cemetery, where he met Sara Landow. They would stand for a long time in front of Sara's sister's grave, and then they would drift up and down the paths, talking. She would lose them when they got into his car and drove away.

The first time she saw them together was a shock, certainly. Sara was as beautifully dressed and as haggard as ever, somehow simultaneously puffy and gaunt, and always pale, so pale. But she smiled at Robert Dwyer, and he touched her arm often when they spoke. Saskia could not imagine how they filled all those hours, or what they found to say to each other, or how Sara managed not to spit in his face. Saskia would not have been able to manage it herself. But Sara was no doubt acting out some redemption fantasy, some passion play of confrontation and forgiveness that helped her get through these days. Saskia would not judge her for that.

Still it was hard to watch them together, the man who had killed her sister and the woman to whom she had shown something of her most private self. Saskia found herself occasionally thinking uncharitable thoughts about Sara. Small slights came back to her—those CD cases, her casual dismissal of Saskia's grief the first time they had met, the way her eyes would take in Saskia's clothes even as they spoke of other things. She was a snob and a narcissist and a drunk.

But Sara was not Saskia's focus. She was peripheral now.

The fourth Sunday after Saskia started following Robert, she didn't go to his house. Instead she rented a car and drove to the cemetery, where she waited until the couple appeared. When they left she was able to follow them all the way to Sara's apartment and watch them go up together. So.

The next bit was surprisingly easy. She hadn't known what to expect, whether she would feel let down after, whether his reaction would disappoint her, whether he would be unmoved, or even laugh. She thought she might bring her sharpest kitchen knife so she could cut him if he laughed. That's what Jenny would have done. Instead he had fallen to his knees and covered his eyes and said *oh god, my god,* and Saskia had suffered him to look at her until his whole body was shaking. She had walked away then feeling like the angel with the flaming sword.

CHAPTER THIRTEEN

Which of them was it who first spoke of suicide? Robert, Sara thought. Almost certainly it was Robert. After that strange evening in her apartment he had begged off their cemetery date the following weekend, and Sara thought perhaps they were done. But he called her a few days later and said he wanted to talk, he needed to talk, was she free?

They met in Stanley Park, near the Rowing Club, and walked the seawall. It was a day of soft edges, grey drizzle, mist on the ocean and shreds of mist caught in the trees, and Robert told her some things he had never told her before. His life came into slightly sharper focus for her, though she said little. He didn't need much prompting.

He had lied to her, he said, about his grandmother. She had committed suicide upon receiving a diagnosis of Alzheimer's. She had waited until they were all out and turned the car on inside the garage. The note she left explained, briefly, that she didn't intend to be a burden.

He had also lied to her about the dog. It hadn't run away. He had kicked it for barking and it had bled internally and died. Its shit had turned black, which he knew meant blood. He had been high at the time, and when he came down he had wanted to die himself.

But what he really wanted to tell her, what he was working towards as they made their way round from the eastern part of the seawall, with its views of the city and the container port and the floating gas stations, to the wilder western side with its sheer cliffs looming over the sea, was about the woman who had died. He didn't know if he had loved her—if that was the right word to describe what had been between them. They had not seen each other often, but when they had the relationship had been intense and at times violent. The accident was in September; her family pulled the plug that Christmas. Grief sent him back to drugs, and by the time he confronted Sara in her office at the University in April he was in terrible shape. He had fought like hell to get his life back after Mattie's death. He had served his time willingly; he had gotten clean. But now he thought he might be losing his mind, because he felt as though the woman he had loved was following him. He kept thinking he was seeing her.

Sara was disappointed that none of these big revelations was about Mattie, but she kept this to herself. Let him talk.

Had she ever heard of such a thing, he wondered? Seeing a dead person everywhere?

Sara thought Dr. Kumar would identify this as yet another manifestation of grief, and said as much. Nothing mysterious or otherworldly, just the brain working a little too hard to process its distress.

But the last time, Robert said, she got close enough that he could smell her perfume. It was her, he knew it was her. The three and a half years since her death disappeared in that breath of perfume.

Sara wondered which perfume, but of course he wouldn't know.

They walked on for a while in silence. Far above them gulls wheeled. It was raining properly now and they encountered few others, only the occasional runner.

Sara remembered something her mother used to say to her about dreams. It didn't matter what the dream was about, her mother claimed, so much as the emotion you came away with.

"How did you feel when you saw her?" Sara asked.

Robert shook his head, and she saw he was near tears.

Sara tried to imagine what it would be like to be faced with Mattie's ghost.

"Did she speak to you?" Sara said. "The woman who died?"

Robert shook his head.

Sara conjured Mattie in her memory, her pink cheeks and blunt nails and the smell of her, baby powder when she had bathed and cumin when she hadn't. She tried to imagine Mattie popping up at bus stops and street corners, hovering just outside the penumbra of a streetlight, but that had not been Mattie's way. She wouldn't have known how to torment anybody, wouldn't have wanted to.

Sara confessed that she spoke to Mattie sometimes, replaying scenes in her head where she had been impatient with her and rewriting those scripts, tipping them to kindness.

"You feel guilty," Robert said.

"Yes. Don't you?"

"About Mattie? You know I do."

"The other woman. Did she have a name, by the way?"

Robert had declined to reveal her name that time, but eventually it came out: Jenny. Of course Sara already knew the name, but she had wanted to see how long it would take him to trust her with it.

The week after he told her Jenny's name, Sara showed up at the cemetery with an armful of lilies. Robert met her at Mattie's grave as usual, but the lilies were not for Mattie. Sara led Robert to a different part of the cem-

etery, where Jennifer Anne Gilbert had a marble headstone next to her parents. Sara gave Robert the lilies,
but he looked stricken, and couldn't move to place
them. "What is this?"

Sara shook her head. "I'm sorry. I thought you knew.
I thought—I thought . . ." Sara realized he was crying,
and then she was crying too. She helped him lay the lilies and then they held each other until they each were
calm again.

"I never knew where she was buried," Robert told her
later, in yet another coffee shop. "It was just a shock,
that's all. I know you meant to be kind."

"You brought flowers for Mattie, that first time." Sara
shook her head. "I wanted to do something nice for you,
for her."

"I ruin everything. Everything I touch, I fuck it up.
Everything."

Sara touched her coffee cup to his. They sat for a
while in silence.

"How did you know where she was?" Robert asked
after a while.

"Google," Sara lied. He nodded.

Now, in the evenings, Robert would pull out a little foil
bit of something and take it to the bathroom, and Sara
wouldn't say anything. Eventually he did his drugs in

front of her. She wasn't sure when exactly he had started using again, but she was pretty sure it was after Jenny had started appearing to him. Every time they hugged goodbye, now, she thought he was waiting to be asked to stay.

Sara confessed she had thought of suicide too. Without Mattie to care for, her life didn't mean a lot. She didn't have much of a purpose. She was tired all the time, and everything was such an effort. After some hesitation she told Robert about her last trip to Paris and how close she had come there. Hesitation because she guessed Paris might as well have been Pluto, to him. He would never see it in this lifetime.

He asked her if she thought there might be an afterlife.

"Where we'll see them again?" she asked, and he nodded. She didn't answer, but thought about Paris. Maybe the afterlife would be like that, little coffees and *quais* and parfumeries and so on. That would be nice.

"I saw her one last time after the accident," Robert was saying. Was this before or after his bit of foil? Had he been talking for a while? Her glass was empty again, but he leaned forward to fill it. "I went to the hospital."

"You said you didn't," Sara said thickly. Did it matter, really? Mattie was still dead. His Jenny was still dead. Talking wouldn't bring them back.

"I know it won't bring them back," Robert said. "That's not why I was telling you. I went to the hospital and snuck into her room. Her eyes were open. She saw me, but she couldn't move."

Sara closed her eyes. Opened them. "What did you do?"

"Whatever I wanted." He began to sob. "I jerked off, okay? She was helpless and it turned me on. I did whatever I wanted, and all she could do was watch."

Sara closed her eyes.

"I didn't think she would die. I didn't know her family would freak out because of what I'd done and take her out of the hospital. That's why she died, because of what I did. If she'd stayed in the hospital, she might have survived. I killed her, okay? It was me."

How tiresome he was, after all. Revelation after revelation, as though his honesty was precious to her when really it was all just Christmas tinsel.

Then they were in her bedroom and he was telling her to lie down. She thought he might get in with her but he tucked her in and sat in the chair in the corner for a long time, watching her. She lay on her back for him, as still as she could, and after a while he left. She heard the snick of the apartment door closing as he let himself out.

Which of them was it who first spoke of suicide? Sara woke the next morning with a dry mouth and a throbbing head. She vomited into the toilet and then she called Robert. "We should just do it. Together. It'll be easier that way."

A long silence. Then: "Yeah."

She hung up and pulled with her fingernails on a rachis spiking out from one of the sofa pillows, and a tiny down feather emerged—sleek as she pulled and then sprung to fluff. Sara let it go and watched it drift in the sunlight for what felt like a long time before it landed on the carpet. That was life, wasn't it? It didn't seem like you were falling.

CHAPTER FOURTEEN

Saskia eased up on Robert Dwyer for a couple of weeks, just to fuck with him. To let him think that maybe, just maybe, it was over. Meantime she went to a salon and bought a wig, straight and honey-coloured, unremarkable. She thought of telling the kindly saleswoman that it was for her sister who was having chemo, but in the end said it was for an audition. The saleswoman didn't care what it was for. She rang up the purchase, and had already turned to the next customer before Saskia had finished putting her wallet away.

The wig let her get closer to him than ever before. She could sit in the same car on the SkyTrain now, and once she scored a booth behind his and Sara's on their maudlin post-graveyard Sunday afternoon coffee date. That day she heard everything. Sara spoke to him in a way that set Saskia's teeth on edge, though it took her a while to figure out why. Sara was frank and funny, and eventually Saskia realized it was because she was speaking to him as a peer. She'd always held a little something back with Saskia, been a little cool, but with Robert she was all warmth. She'd really gone all in.

Well then, Saskia thought.

On her way home, she wadded the wig into a ball and dropped it into a dumpster in the parkade below her building.

The next time Saskia saw Robert Dwyer it was at night. She had thought about wearing the dog collar and leash but she wasn't looking for opera, and the collar—though distressing to her in its own way—wasn't what she held against him. Enough with the ghost bullshit.

Instead, she used Jenny's phone to text him a photo and then a message.

He showed up at the empty parking lot she'd chosen for their rendezvous looking pale but determined. "You're the sister," he said immediately. "I'm so fucking stupid. I should have figured it out."

Saskia didn't say anything, because she realized in that moment that the sound of her voice would be the sound of Jenny's voice to him, and perhaps that would be a gift.

"Why are you following me? What do you want?"

She stepped closer to him, and she saw him will himself not to flinch. Closer; close enough to touch, to smell, to hold.

He said, "I miss her too, okay? I wish she was still alive."

"So you could hurt her some more?"

She saw her voice do what she had feared. His body opened to it and his eyes softened. His voice went rough. "I never did anything she didn't ask for." His eyes went down her and up again. "She mentioned a sister, but never that you were twins." Down, up. "What do you want?"

"I wanted to take a look at you. We didn't have secrets, but she kept you a secret. I wanted to see you for myself."

He shook his head. "You're a real little mindfucker."

"You knew she wasn't well, right?" Saskia said. "Of course you knew. You knew you could get her to do anything you wanted. That was part of her sickness."

"I have no fucking idea what you're talking about. I tried to make her happy. You know she wasn't a happy person, right? You know she hated your parents? Your mom was a drunk and your dad was a bully. Yeah, she told me shit about your family. But you, you." Down, up. "She said the two of you were strangers. She said even though you lived in the same house, you didn't know her and she didn't know you and she didn't see that ever changing. You needed her for everything and she was so fucking tired of you. Tired of being smarter than you and prettier and more successful. Tired of being tied to you. She wouldn't even tell me your name. How about that?"

But of course that was wrong. Saskia was the one who had been tired.

"When I heard about the accident I went to the hospital but they wouldn't let me see her. Because I wasn't family. She could have you sick fucks around her but not me. She wanted me there, I know she did. I knew what she wanted better than she did."

"You went to the hospital?"

He shook his head. "Of course I fucking went to the fucking hospital."

"The man who assaulted her. That was you."

"Assaulted." He looked at her wonderingly. "You really are the dumb twin, aren't you?"

"What would you call it?"

"I knew what she liked. Maybe you're not so different from her after all. That's why you're really here, isn't it? You're not angry—you're curious. You want a taste."

"No."

"Sure you do. What's your name?"

"Leave me alone."

"Leave *you* alone? No, that's not what you want. I know what you want."

He grabbed her hair and pulled her head back so she had to look up at him. "I put some on her tongue when

I was done," he said. "She was still sexy to me. I wanted her to know that. I gave her a gift none of you could give her, that no one could take away."

"A gift," Saskia repeated.

"I didn't pity her. I didn't treat her any different. What's your name?"

"Saskia. My name's Saskia."

"It's nice to meet you, Saskia. Here's what's going to happen. I'm going to let go, and I'm going to leave. It's my rules now. Understand?"

Saskia nodded.

He let go and brushed his hands off. A few of her dark hairs drifted to the ground. "You follow me again, I'm going to assume you want some more."

Saskia took a step forward. She put her hand on his chest, over his heart, and leaned so close that her hair brushed his cheek. "You'd like that," she whispered in his ear.

They stood close and still for a long moment.

"I blamed you for killing her," Saskia murmured. "For a long time. You sent the last text she ever read, right before the accident, and I thought that was the only puzzle piece that fit. But I was wrong. You know who really killed her?"

She inclined her face a little so he could see her eyes.

"Me," she said. "I'm the one who told the hospital to

let her go. My parents couldn't make the decision, but I could. I sat with her and I told her what we were going to do. I don't think she could hear me, but I told her anyway, just in case. I wanted her to know it was me."

His face had gone white.

"Just like I want you to know it was me."

He took a step back, stumbled, found his feet.

"You'll see me again," she said.

CHAPTER FIFTEEN

They met at the cemetery gate at 4:00 p.m. on Sunday afternoon. It was a relatively busy time, with a service just concluding and many visitors. They went first to Jennifer Anne Gilbert's grave, as they had agreed. Sara hung back while Robert knelt down, touched the stone, and spoke too quietly for her to hear. Then he rose and rejoined her and they walked to *Martha Ellen Landow, 1977–2016.*

They had argued about this, but Sara was adamant. Mattie was what connected them. It had to be Mattie.

Sara had done the research and brought the supplies. They had talked about Sara going first, but Robert had looked at her with such eyes that she said she didn't mind if he wanted to get it over with.

"I'm afraid," he confessed. "Not of this. But if our timing's off and you leave me alone."

"I won't leave you alone."

She took a piece of plastic tarp from her tote bag and laid out the picnic. They sat down together before Mattie's grave. It was a dry day, luckily. On a rainy day they might have looked odd sitting this way.

He took the antiemetics with a few sips from a bottle of water and ate all of the little ham sandwich she had made him. The pills he took doggedly with a mickey of vodka, his preference. For herself she had brought a half-bottle of wine. She had read of nightmare scenarios, the wishful dead who had to be finished with a plastic bag or pillow, or who vomited up the pills and then had to eat their own vomit to get them down again. But he had no such trouble. After a few minutes he said, "Now you." Already he was slurring and his breathing was shallow.

Sara didn't move.

"Sara," he said thickly. She turned to look at him, to let him see her face. "Sara." He slumped forward as the forty Seconals swamped his body. "Don't leave me."

Sara got up and brushed off her skirt. She picked up her tote bag. Robert Dwyer tried to reach her, tried to stop her. His fingertips brushed her skirt, but he could no longer grip. "No," he whispered.

Sara walked away.

At the gates she looked back. He had slumped over onto the grave, but in all the time she had been visiting the cemetery Sara had seen much odd behaviour dictated by grief and she guessed that anyone seeing him would only give him space. In the unlikely event that someone had noticed the two of them together, Sara could say she had sought him out as part of her therapy. Donna August would vouch for that because Sara had told her as much, months ago.

Across the street, Saskia leaned against a tree. She was back to her old self, in boots and jeans and a drab rain jacket of some depressingly practical technical fabric. They nodded to each other. Sara walked to the bus stop. Behind her, Saskia would be heading into the cemetery. She would sit with him now, as they had agreed. That would make his prostration over the grave even less suspicious. Anyway, Saskia had wanted to see the end. She would have another half hour or so with him before he lost consciousness, and then several more hours' watch after that until he died. Sara didn't need to know how she planned to use that time.

The bus was crowded, and Sara was forced to stand all the way back into town. By the time she got off the bus she felt so exhausted that she ducked into the nearest café for a cup of tea to fortify her for the walk back to her apartment. Needing tea to walk three blocks—that was age tapping her on the shoulder. The windows of the café were steamy. She thought she might stop for a box of dandan noodles to eat in front of an old movie. Myrna Loy and William Powell, maybe. A quiet night in.

CHAPTER SIXTEEN

July 2019

After the suicide of Robert Dwyer, Saskia called Fen. "So soon?" Fen said.

"I've decided to travel."

Even though it had only been a few months, Saskia made a profit on the sale of the condo—that was Vancouver for you. She took Jenny's clothes and the kitchenware to a women's shelter. She kept Jenny's phone and her mother's sapphire engagement ring, and she downloaded her father's favourite music from iTunes.

"Twenty-seven," the man next to her on the plane said. "Oh, to be twenty-seven again. You've got your whole life in front of you."

Saskia put in her earbuds. The ocean from this height was dull, reminding her of the skin that forms on hot milk. She felt she could reach down and with the touch of a finger pull away the surface of the sea.

———

London was muggy daytime after the twilight of the plane. Saskia took the Tube to the National Gallery to eat a salad and kill time before her appointment that evening.

The pub he had chosen—the Silver Cross, south of Trafalgar Square—was cozy but unremarkable. It had flagstones and wingback chairs and seemed to be staffed entirely by Australians. She recognized his long, aging-rock-star hair from the back. She thought about the fact that he had elected to present himself to her this way, to let her see him before he saw her. She touched his shoulder. "Professor Taillac."

He turned, stood, took the hand she held out to shake and pulled her in to press each of his cheeks to hers. "Michel," he said.

"Michel."

He went to the bar and returned with a couple of pints.

"Why here?" Saskia asked a little while later. "Why not Paris?" For he did seem very French in this very English place. A parody, almost. The barkeep had mocked his accent so viciously that Saskia understood he was a regular and they liked each other quite well.

"I did initially retire there," Michel Taillac admitted.

"But it didn't fit me anymore. My family are dead or moved away, and my old friends have all moved on, in their different ways." He shrugged. "I found it lonely. So much has changed there, and my memories are important to me. I didn't want them overlaid with what Paris has become, so that I would no longer be able to distinguish what belonged to me and what did not. London, for me, has no such associations. It is very clean in my mind."

"There was never a question of remaining in Vancouver?"

A wave of the hand. "I am European. I have more than enough money to spend the rest of my days indulging in my own particular comforts. Vancouver"—he leaned forward and lowered his voice—"is very boring."

Saskia laughed. He leaned back, surprised, pleased. She caught his eyes flickering across her body, and knew he would go to bed happy that night because he had, maybe for one of the last times in his life, made a woman give way to pleasure.

She wiped her eyes and they touched glasses. "If only you knew."

They spoke for another hour, about the books he was reading and the exhibition she had seen that afternoon, which he had also seen. He asked about her plans.

"I've decided to go back to school, actually. Law school."

"I didn't know that was an interest of yours."

"My father was a lawyer. He always wanted me to join his practice, but I was too close to it. Or too close to him. It feels less fraught, now that he's gone. Real estate law, maybe. I seem to have a knack for real estate. I start in September, anyway." Saskia had not slept on the plane, and exhaustion began its wash. She yawned and yawned again.

"How long are you in London?" Michel Taillac asked.

She intuited he would suggest they meet again. "Just tonight. I'm going to be in Italy, mostly." From her bag she withdrew the book he had given her at their last meeting and set it on the table between them. "I contacted you because I wanted to return this."

"Ah." She waited until both their fingers were touching the cover before releasing it. He said, "What did you think?"

"Honestly, I was expecting some kind of filth." Saskia watched him brush his fingers over the title, tracing the letters one by one, reclaiming his treasure as he listened to her. "Some kind of *sadisme, dégradation.* I only opened it for the first time very recently."

"Me and my little bookcase of the forbidden." Their eyes met. "All sound and fury, I'm afraid. I did enjoy my reputation while it lasted, though. And?"

"It's extraordinary." *Romances of the Petty Christ* was its faded golden title, and beneath that, *translated by a*

Gentlewoman. The gentlewoman, according to the Victorian foreword, was a sixteenth-century Florentine lady, a sheltered autodidact who had found in her father's library this medieval manuscript and translated it, to pass the time, from French (her fourth language) into English (her fifth). The translation was halting and clumsy ("petty" for *petit,* as an example). Nonetheless the stories were of an ethereal sweetness, otherworldly gnostic tales of the childhood of the Saviour. A modern afterword to the book explained that the actual author was an inmate of a Louisiana mental asylum in the nineteen-fifties, a young woman who did not otherwise speak or communicate and had been thought at the time to be an idiot. She had written the romances on the inside of her hospital robes, where they remained undiscovered until the undertaker removed her clothing to bathe her for the grave. There was no Victorian foreword or medieval French manuscript or Florentine gentlewoman. The whole Borgesian project came from the troubled mind of this young woman who died in her late twenties.

"An extraordinary number of contradictions to reconcile," Michel Taillac said. "And an extraordinary number of lives for one life to contain. It stretches credibility, doesn't it? Still, I find it comforting, *sa foi.* Her faith." He stopped tapping and pushed it back towards her. "You should keep it."

"Why?"

He held her gaze for a long moment, then excused himself to the washroom. It was a quarter of an hour before she realized he wasn't coming back.

Outside it was early evening. After-work crowds surged around her. At a newsagent's down the street she bought a postage-paid cardboard pouch. From her bag she took the other book, Christine Bouchard's, sealed it inside, and addressed it. She dropped it into a nearby postbox. Without much thought, she let Jenny tip Michel Taillac's book and note in after it.

CHAPTER SEVENTEEN

August 2019

On the third anniversary of Mattie's death, Sara made a little picnic of nice things: cambozola on a baguette, cornichons, cherries, strawberries. She spent considerable time choosing the wine, eventually deciding on both a crémant and a rosé from the Languedoc. Choosing the right rose perfume took even longer. She wore her palest blue linen dress and the Alaïa sandals, and carried the white silk shawl in her bag for her shoulders in case it cooled down later.

Sara's leave had ended in early May. Though she was not scheduled to teach again until September, there'd been much to keep her busy at the University—letters of reference, course prep, peer reviews, digitization of the student thesis library. This last had consisted of overseeing a summer work-learn student, an immensely tall young man who was writing a thesis about the ethical implications of identity theft, who spent hours at the department scanner, earbuds cemented in. She had tried to chat with him a couple of times but it was a lost cause. He would smile patiently and nod and never move to take the earbuds out. He'd reminded her of Saskia.

She had waited, after Robert Dwyer's suicide, for the phone call, the knock at the door, the uniform and the boots and *down to the station for a few questions*, but it never came.

She was alone now, utterly alone.

She knew nothing of Saskia's plans. That had been the arrangement. Saskia knew nothing of hers. And so Sara had spent the summer enjoying summer's gifts: the lengthening days, a few good books, an early music concert. She went coffee-and-shopping with Donna August. She'd thought about David Park, but when she said the testing words to herself—*never again*—she felt nothing. So be it.

At the cemetery, she swept Jenny's gravestone and placed a bouquet of larkspur just so. She brushed her fingertips along Jenny's name.

Mattie's stone was dusty and looked neglected. Sara spent a few minutes washing and weeding before she spread her blanket and laid out her picnic. She took the first tablet with the crémant and ate the food, a little doggedly towards the end.

She closed her eyes to listen to a lone gull exulting, way up there in the blue.

The cork in the rosé gave her a bit of trouble. For a few moments she wondered if her whole plan would fall through because she had been too much of a snob to buy a screw top.

A NOTE ABOUT THE AUTHOR

Annabel Lyon is the author of seven books for adults and kids, including the internationally bestselling *The Golden Mean*. She teaches Creative Writing at the University of British Columbia.

A NOTE ON THE TYPE

This book was set in Janson, a typeface named for
the Dutchman Anton Janson, but is actually the work
of Nicholas Kis (1650–1702). The type is an excellent
example of the influential and sturdy Dutch types that
prevailed in England up to the time William Caslon
(1692–1766) developed his own incomparable designs
from them.

Typeset by Scribe
Allentown, Pennsylvania

Printed and bound by Berryville Graphics
Berryville, Virginia